THE ICE MAIDEN'S TALE

THE ICE MAIDEN'S TALE

Lisa Preziosi

Xist Publishing

Xist Publishing
PO Box 61593
Irvine, CA 92602
www.xistpublishing.com

Publisher's Note: This is a work of fiction. Names, characters, places, and incidents are a product of the author's imagination. Locales and public names are sometimes used for atmospheric purposes. Any resemblance to actual people, living or dead, or to businesses, companies, events, institutions, or locales is completely coincidental.

Ordering Information:
Quantity sales. Special discounts are available on quantity purchases by corporations, associations, and others. For details, contact the "Special Sales Department" at the address above.

The Ice Maiden's Tale/ Lisa Preziosi -- 1st ed.
ISBN 978-1-5324-0231-9
eISBN: 978-1-5324-0232-6

For my Nonna, Maria Preziosi
For my Papa, Dante Preziosi
For my Zio, Anthony Preziosi
&
my Zio, Mario Preziosi

You are forever carved into my memory.

"I saw an angel in the marble, and I carved until

I set him free..."

—Michelangelo

PROLOGUE

Every town has its own witch. Sometimes she's stooped over and has tufts of white hair, other times a long charcoal braid and perfect posture, but no matter how well disguised she is, children can always spot her. In twelve-year-old Johanna Sullivan's neighborhood of Dunkler Wald, the resident witch was named Mrs. Kinder and she lived across the street.

The sky was overcast and as gray as pigeon feathers, when Johanna rounded the corner toward Mrs. Kinder's house. Pulling her younger brother Casper in tow, she trudged up the creaky stairs. They bowed beneath the children's weight, giving the unsettling feeling that at any moment the kids would crash right through the old wood.

Mrs. Kinder's house slumped against itself, like all the wood was resting and being held up only by the wispy cobwebs in its corners. The paint was peeling and chipped; the windows dark and covered with heavy drapes. Dangling from the sagging porch beams were rusted baskets so grimy, the flowers had long since abandoned them. The baskets blew in the wind, giving out a long, whiny sound that sent spidery shivers down Johanna's neck.

"Why, *why*, do we have to go?" whined Casper.

"Because Mom said we do," answered Johanna, pulling Casper along.

"But *why*? Did Mom finally decided to kill us?" Casper exclaimed, his eyes narrowing at Johanna.

Casper, Johanna's annoying nine-year-old brother, was frequently suspicious of others. He had brown hair and green eyes that narrowed whenever he thought someone was trying to trick him which, of course, was most of the time.

"It's only for a couple hours."

"*Hours!*" Casper whined. "But I *hate* it there, her house smells like mothballs and basement and…and wet cat!"

Johanna sighed, "Casper, you know Mrs. Kinder doesn't have a cat."

"Exactly!" Casper answered, raising an eyebrow. "What does that tell you?"

Johanna let out another sigh and used her sternest I'm-your-big-sister-and-Mom-left-me-in-charge-so-you-have-to-listen-to-me voice. "This isn't my favorite way to spend an afternoon either, but we have to do what Mom says. Now hurry up before someone sees us going inside."

As they stepped on the old, creaky porch, a bolt of lightning cracked the sky like an egg. Rain poured out. Johanna screamed.

"Yeah right," replied Casper. "This house doesn't bother you at all. You're not even a little bit scared." He punctuated his sentence by sticking out his tongue.

"The lightning just surprised me okay? Now let's get this over with." Johanna approached the front door. It must have been painted red once, but now all that was left were grimy patches of paint on the old wood. Just above Johanna's eyes was a rusted door knocker. She guessed that it was supposed to be an angelic face, like those cute golden cherubs you see scattered inside Christmas trees, but time and weather had battered it, making it look ill and ghostly.

Johanna took a deep breath and grabbed the knocker, trying not to look at the haunting face.

Quickly she rapped it against the door. It let out a surprisingly loud boom.

"Why can't she get a doorbell like a normal person?" Johanna grumbled.

"Because she's a *witch*," Casper replied smacking himself in the forehead. "How many times do I have to tell you?"

"And how many times do I have to tell you that she's just a strange, old lady—"

With that, the door creaked open, and in the doorway, stood the aforementioned Mrs. Kinder. She was one of the tiniest and most ancient looking people Johanna had ever seen. She couldn't have been more than four and a half feet tall. Her hair was wound in two braids on top of her head, like a gray crown, and perched on her nose were oddly small spectacles. Peering over them were blue eyes that seemed ghostly bright against her skin.

Her mouth broke into a smile that seemed almost too large for her little, wrinkled face. "Welcome dearies! Come right in, I've made you some apricot cookies."

When Mrs. Kinder turned her back Casper mouthed to Johanna, "Don't eat the cookies." Then he grabbed his throat and faked choking.

"Stop," Johanna mouthed back and followed Mrs. Kinder into the house. Johanna would never admit it out loud, but Casper was right about the smell in Mrs.

Kinder's house, exactly like wet cat and moth balls. The entryway had an old oriental rug the color of dried blood and covered in black swirls. There was a narrow winding staircase ahead with stained glass windows opposite its twisted railing.

"We're not going up there?" Casper exclaimed in horror.

Johanna glowered at him.

"Of course not, Casper. I thought we'd go into the sitting room for a story," answered Mrs. Kinder in her high-pitched voice.

"Story?" Casper eeked out, his eyes narrowing once again. "Can't we just watch TV?"

"I don't own a television," Mrs. Kinder replied and Casper gasped.

"But—but—how? How do you live?" Casper asked incredulously.

"If you mean how I pass the time, dearie, I have lots of hobbies."

At that, Johanna gulped a bit. The word *hobbies* seemed so ominous. Knitting and reading were not the first things that came to Johanna's mind. Instead, she pictured the witch from Hansel and Gretel fattening up the children in sweet anticipation of eating them. Casper gave Johanna an I-told-you-she-was–a-witch-but-you-didn't-believe-me-and-now-we're-going-to-die glare.

"This way, children." Mrs. Kinder motioned through an archway, just right of the staircase. In the center of the sitting room, there was an antique style couch and chairs--the kind that children are almost never allowed to sit on, which is fine with most children as they are terribly uncomfortable anyway. Between the couch and chairs, was a dark wood coffee table with a blue glass dish piled high with strange, yellow cookies flecked with red.

The first thing Casper noticed was the overabundance of pink everywhere: pink wallpaper, a pink floral rug, dark pink drapes—everything in this room screamed out "little old lady's house." Casper's eyes narrowed. Even if there wasn't a cauldron, or a rack of strange potions, he was sure, that Mrs. Kinder was, in fact, a witch.

The first thing Johanna noticed was that the entire back wall was a floor to ceiling bookshelf brimming with all kinds of books. The books seemed very old, and Johanna fought the urge to run over and pick one up.

"Have a seat and help yourself to some cherry apricot cookies," Mrs. Kinder said. "Would you both like some milk, or perhaps some cocoa?"

"I'm fine," Casper answered a little quickly, as he sat down on the sofa. Johanna sat down next to him and gave him a sharp look.

"I'll have some cocoa and I'm sure Casper will want some too." Johanna replied.

"Wonderful!" Mrs. Kinder exclaimed clapping her hands together. "I'll be back in a moment, make yourselves comfortable."

"What have you done?" Casper hissed. "We're gonna drink that and turn into ants or something!"

"It's cocoa, Casper. Not poison. Relax. Mom would want us to behave—and we don't want to upset her with everything going on. *Please.*"

"Fine. And when we're both turned into toads or frogs, you'll see I was right," Casper answered.

Johanna rose from the couch and went over to the bookshelf.

"What are you doing?" Casper asked.

"I just want to see what kind of books these are—"

"They're witch books! Leave them alone."

Johanna looked over the books. They were all leather bound with faded titles. Some were thick, others quite slim. The writing on them seemed odd, but before Johanna could examine one closely, Mrs. Kinder returned.

She placed a tray with three pink mugs on the table. "Here you go dearies." Mrs. Kinder noticed Johanna by the bookshelf. "Do you like stories?" she asked Johanna, raising one tiny eyebrow.

"Yes, very much." Johanna replied, feeling an odd sensation in her belly.

"Perfect. I've got just the story for you both. Come sit." Johanna returned to the couch and Mrs. Kinder walked over to the bookshelf.

"Thanks *so* much, Johanna!" Casper whispered.

Mrs. Kinder's back was blocking a portion of the shelf and Johanna couldn't see which book she chose. When she returned, she held in her hand, a golden leather book. It was faded and a bit grimy, but somehow the binding seemed to shine. Johanna didn't remember seeing it on the shelf.

Mrs. Kinder settled herself in the chair across from the children and cracked open the book. She adjusted her spectacles, ever so slightly, then caressed the page with her wrinkled fingers.

"In our world, when magic happens outside of a storybook, we call it a miracle. And miracles are considered so rare and special that lifetimes can go by without so much as a hint of one. But there are faraway places where our kind of miracles are as common as blades of grass in an open field. In the northern region of one of these worlds, in the top far east corner, past green forests, swamps, lakes, and even an ocean, there lived a young artist named Gabriel."

"What kind of artist was he?" asked Johanna.

"He was a sculptor," Mrs. Kinder continued. "He carved all kinds of statues. Sometimes in stone, other times in wood, he'd spend hour after hour carving until every last detail was perfect."

"He lived alone in a small cabin at the bottom of a snowy mountain near the Frozen Forest. This region lived in everlasting winter—seasons never changed, flowers never blossomed and the ice never melted. It's not the sort of place most people would make their home, but Gabriel had spent his boyhood there and couldn't remember traveling farther than a few miles from it."

"What else did he do? Did he join with pirates and look for treasure?" Casper interrupted.

"He spent his time walking in the Frozen Forest, searching for something. And before you ask me what he was looking for, you have to understand that sometimes people search for things without really knowing what they're seeking."

"There were two things he prized above all others," Mrs. Kinder held up two fingers for emphasis. "Any guesses as to what they might be?"

"Pirate treasure!" Casper called out.

"A magic book," Johanna added hopefully.

"The first was a heavy old chisel that belonged to his grandfather. The other item is a bit harder to guess—"

"Pirate treasure!" Casper interrupted again.

"It's not pirate treasure," Johanna sighed.

"It was an old fiddle that had been in Gabriel's family for as long as he could remember."

"What's so important about an old fiddle?" Casper asked, with a sour voice, partially because he'd been scolded and sighed at, and partially because he was realizing there might not be pirate treasure in the story.

Before Johanna could let out another sigh, Mrs. Kinder answered. "When Gabriel was just a little boy, rough winds shook the walls of his home and sounded like the shrieking of banshees he'd heard about in old ghost stories. To drown out the wailing and his fear, Gabriel played the fiddle. Like all things worth doing, it took time and practice for him to play melodies instead of just ill-tuned squealing, but as he grew to adulthood his songs became beautiful—not quite as beautiful as his carvings, but still lovely."

"This isn't a very good story." Casper complained.

"Casper!" Johanna exclaimed in embarrassment.

Mrs. Kinder laughed. "That's because I'm not even at the story part yet, but it's high time we get started. This story doesn't begin, the way you think it might and the way most stories do. It doesn't begin with a big adventure or a journey, or even pirate treasure. It starts with a tiny choice—one that seems unremarkable at the time, but that changes the course of destiny. One crisp morning, our Gabriel decided to search for firewood—and it's with that simple decision that our tale begins."

1

THE SCULPTOR & THE SORCERER

As Gabriel walked through the Frozen Forest, ice-covered branches crunched beneath his boots and his breath made white swirls in the air. All the trees in the forest were so thick with frost, not even the fiercest wind could move their limbs. No animals stirred and there was no noise, save the sound of Gabriel's footsteps. The forest was as cold and lifeless as an ice cube.

Gabriel pulled his patched cloak against him and went deeper into the forest. He had long since grown accustomed to the snowdrifts and gusts of freezing wind and couldn't remember a time when he'd stepped outside into warmth. Eventually, he came to a clearing where some trees had fallen. Their long branches lay tangled in a stack a bit taller than Gabriel.

"Maybe some of the branches on the bottom will be less icy," he said, trying to add a note of cheerfulness to his voice. It was Gabriel's habit to talk to himself. He found that talking aloud made him feel as though someone else was there. Gabriel pushed several trees out of the way, and realized they had been covering something.

"What's this?" he asked aloud. Struggling, he slowly moved more tree limbs. Once those were out of the way, a cave entrance was revealed. Peering inside, Gabriel saw only shadows. He stepped closer. "Is anyone there?" he asked. The only response was his own echo.

Curious, Gabriel crept inside. Gray stone surrounded him and a long, narrow passageway snaked out ahead. The sound of water dripping resonated throughout the cave. The more he walked, the less light there was. The darkness became so deep he could feel it pressing against his face. Gabriel fought back a shiver. "Why are you doing this?" he whispered to himself. "You're not the adventurous kind. And at the very least you could have gotten a torch first. If you're going to end up breakfast for some beast, at least you'll see him coming. Unless of course, he's hibernating and

your incessant chattering wakes him up." Gabriel
sighed at himself in disgust and was just about to turn
back, when he came to a sharp corner and found himself in a larger, open space. Here, sunlight shone
through cracks in the rock and sparkled off the ice that
ran in frozen rivers along the cave walls. It was like
being inside a mirror.

In the center, stood a huge block of ice, formed by
water that had dripped through the top of the cave. A
golden light seemed to emanate from the center of the
ice. As Gabriel moved closer, the light grew brighter
and somehow more golden. Quickly, he pulled off his
glove, wanting to touch the ice and see if it was as
warm as it looked. He placed his hand against it, and
the moment his warm palm touched the frozen block,
the light swirled into a face, like that of an angel, staring back at him---a face with eyes sadder than any he
could have imagined.

His mouth opened in a gasp, but no sound
emerged. His eyes widened and he stopped hearing the
sounds of the cave, or the frantic beating of his own
heart. Gabriel's mind couldn't form a thought beyond
the vision. It was the very thing he had been looking
for. Suddenly, the golden glow grew unbearably bright,
and Gabriel couldn't stop himself from blinking.
When his eyes opened again, the face was gone.

"Come back!" He cried out with a force that surprised him. Anguish overtook him, so great, that he didn't notice the pain spreading through his now red and nearly frozen hand. Instead of pulling away from the ice, he brought his other hand up, moving both of them back and forth against the surface, as if that would summon the vision back. "Did I imagine it?" Gabriel asked himself. "Was she some kind of ghost— or just a trick of the light?"

Gabriel brought his face close to the ice and gazed intently, but it was only frozen water—no light, no face, no angel; nothing at all but ice. Despite the lack of any angelic presence or even the faintest bit of light, Gabriel was unable to pull away. So he waited, hoping the vision would appear again.

Gabriel stood so long the daylight shifted to pink sunset, then to blue moonlight. Eventually he was shivering so violently, he had no choice but to leave. He returned to his little cabin with a heavy heart, feeling as though he was carrying the weight of the entire mountain in his chest.

He tried to settle in for the night. He warmed some broth to eat, but it tasted like wet sawdust in his mouth. He cleaned the little cabin—putting away his tools, sweeping up the dust, and lining the fire logs in a neat stack. He even stitched the fraying patches on his old cloak. When he had finished, Gabriel was no more tired than when he began. "What's wrong with you?" he asked himself. "Why can't you sit still?" He paced the wood floorboards and stared at the crackling fire that burned hot in the stone fireplace. "There had to be someone in the ice," Gabriel said. "I could never have imagined such a face."

He looked above the mantle, at the old fiddle that hung there. It was worn and faded in the way that only things well loved can be. Gabriel's hands felt odd to him now, as though something had changed in them after he'd touched the ice. He reached over and grabbed the instrument, longing for its familiar comfort, hoping that the feel of wood and string against his fingers would ease this unexpected despair. He placed the fiddle at his chin and lifted the bow.

The note resonated softly at first, then so loudly it made the windows rattle. The melody that took shape was dark and cold and sounded the way bitter rain feels against your skin. His fingers moved in a frantic rhythm as though trying to escape the pain that overflowed his heart and spilled out through the strings. The strings spun a stinging dance, the notes as sharp and cold as icicles. Gabriel's bow moved violently in one last flourish and with a crashing final note, the song ended.

He stood very still for a moment and took a deep breath. "Congratulations Gabriel, you've finally gone mad. All it took was seeing one frost-bitten angel. Your imagination has finally gotten the best of you. She wasn't real, just forget her." Despite his words, Gabriel was trembling, and felt as though a chill had crept into his bones. He returned the fiddle and bow to their resting places. Becoming aware of how tired and heavy his body felt, he went to his narrow bed.

That night in his sleep, he tossed and turned, dreaming of disappearing angels, mysterious music, and the sound of fluttering wings. The last thing he remembered was a voice unlike any he'd heard before, repeating three simple words: *Set. Me. Free*.

Gabriel awoke long before the night had ended and jumped out of bed. "I understand now," he said. He grabbed his favorite chisel, a hammer, and a pick, threw them into a satchel along with some food, then set out for the cave.

By the blue light of the moon spilling into the cavern, Gabriel set to work upon the ice. Day and night he labored, stopping only to eat a few bites for supper. He worked so hard his hands grew raw and bloody. He slept so little that he would collapse from exhaustion, and wake up shivering and alone on the cavern floor. But still he kept chiseling away, trying to somehow free the angel in the ice.

At last, one dark night, he was finished. It was a lady, too perfect to be real, and too real to be perfect. She had a delicate face with gentle eyes, but for all her beauty, she seemed the very definition of sadness; as though her soul had been carved from sorrow itself.

Gabriel stared at his creation, "Did I really make you?" he asked. In awe, he studied the graceful line of her neck and the melancholy slant of her mouth. She seemed more real than anything he'd carved before.

"You're done. There's nothing more for me to do. I'm finished—you're—you're finished." Gabriel glanced down at his hands and then back at the statue. "But if we're both finished, why don't I want to leave?" Gabriel had been so sure that if he completed the statue, the despair would leave him and his life would be just as it had been before. He had been convinced that if he freed the angel, he'd be able to forget her perfect face. But alas, our poor Gabriel was wrong, and the odd sadness that had filled him, did not leave.

He paced for hours. "Haven't I done just what you asked me to do? " he whispered hoarsely, his voice strained. "Didn't I set you free?"

And of course the ice maiden didn't answer. She was just a block of ice, after all, the most beautiful block of ice in the whole world, but still, just ice. "I don't have anything else to give you," he continued, his voice a thin whisper. "So please leave me in peace now." With those words, Gabriel turned his back and left the cave. As dark took the sky and the stars awoke, he made his way back to the cabin.

Again he tried to sleep, hoping the curious dreams would leave him now. But once again he tossed and turned, dreaming of haunted eyes the color of ice. Awaking abruptly, he grabbed his wool cloak and fiddle and returned to the cave. He stood staring at his lady. Who was she? And what did she want from him?

"Why do you haunt me?" he asked, the words echoing throughout the cavern. "It's like we're connected in some strange way. But I'm real and you're not. I thought if I freed you, that if I made you what you wanted to be, then you'd let me go." Gabriel shook his head. "But still you haunt my dreams. What else can I do for you? Is there something that you long for? Or are you just lonely?" Gabriel gazed at her intently and his voice softened. "I understand loneliness. Sometimes I feel as though I'm the only person in this entire world. You're the closest I've come to anyone, in a very long time, and you're not even real."

Gabriel looked down at his fiddle. "When I feel most alone, I play music. Somehow it helps. I know I'm crazy for coming here—even crazier for talking to a block of ice, but I thought I'd play us both a song and maybe the night would seem less lonely."

It was a slow song filled with longing. The notes that floated from the strings perfumed the air with hopes too dear to express in words. It was a song of loneliness and of wanting, as though Gabriel were reaching out his hand and waiting for someone to grasp it. Then quite suddenly, the song was over.

He looked at his lady again, so perfect in her stillness, so unmoved by his music. "Goodnight, fair maiden," he whispered, and silently stole away. That night Gabriel finally slept peacefully, dreaming of lilting music and melting ice.

Night after night, he returned to play to the ice maiden. Each time he played, he wondered if there was a soul trapped behind those crystal eyes. Was there really a spirit there who demanded her sorrow be appeased with a song?

After the seventh night, he returned to his lonely cabin, and laid himself on his bed. This time he dreamt the statue was flesh and blood. There was color in her face, a smile on her lips, and her hair flowed in the wind. She wasn't still; she wasn't frozen. She reached for his hand, but something unseen stopped her, and when she couldn't touch him, she began to cry. Her tears streamed down her face and onto her billowing gown, leaving an icy trail. In a few moments, she was completely frozen again.

Gabriel woke with a great ache deep inside him, as though someone had taken a pick to his heart and cracked it down the center. He grabbed his fiddle and ran to the cavern.

Panting and out of breath, he arrived at the cave. Standing there in the cold emptiness, he stared at the lady in the ice. As if in mockery of his dream, she remained unbearably still.

"Enough." Gabriel said. "I can't spend my life haunted, thinking of a lady who can't speak, or feel, or even breathe. Who doesn't even exist! Before I saw you, I was content with my life, or at least it was bearable. I was accustomed to my loneliness, you see. As accustomed as anyone is, I suppose. I kept busy looking after my cabin and I filled the emptiness with music and carving. But now--" emotion clogged Gabriel's voice and he paused for a moment. "Now I can't sleep, I—I haven't carved anything since you. My whole world has become painful dreams and sad songs. There's only one thing left for me to do." Gabriel picked up his fiddle to play.

The song started, but it was different this time. It was the melody of goodbye, a song almost sad enough to melt ice. Almost. There were no words to his farewell—he couldn't have found the words if he tried. And so he kept on playing the bittersweet song of things that can never be. And then it ended.

Gabriel gave the ice maiden one last, long look, as if to carve her face in his memory. Without hesitation, he placed the fiddle at her feet. And then, he was gone.

"Gabriel left the Frozen Forest and headed south to the warmer, distant lands he'd heard about in stories." Mrs. Kinder continued. "Another traveler was moving in the opposite direction and heading toward the Frozen Forest. Sebastian moved from place to place, never staying anywhere for very long. What made Sebastian different from other travelers was that he was a gifted sorcerer—"

"Magic! *Finally*, something interesting in this story." Casper grumbled.

"So Casper, magic interests you?" Mrs. Kinder asked.

Casper's eyes narrowed in response to Mrs. Kinder's tone, and he thought it wise to answer her question very carefully. "I like stories about magic if that's what you mean."

Mrs. Kinder laughed. "If you had magical powers, what kind of things would you do?"

"I'd make myself a magical pirate ship and look for treasure, of course." Casper answered quite matter-of-factly.

Johanna rolled her eyes and responded in her you're-just-my-annoying-immature-little-brother tone. "*Always* with the pirate ships."

"How many times do I have to tell you—it's cause they're *always* cool," Casper answered with his I-don't-care-what-you-say-cause-you're-stupid voice.

"Well, I'd heal all the sick people in the world." Johanna answered quickly. "And I'd—I'd make it so puppies could stay little, that way you could have a dog even if you lived in a very tiny house."

Mrs. Kinder shook her head at this exchange and chuckled to herself. "So, what do you think the sorcerer did? And no Casper, he didn't make himself a pirate ship."

"He helped people who needed it? Like when people perform miracles?" Johanna said.

"I'm afraid you'll be disappointed, dearie."

"Hah!" said Casper. "You're not so smart either, Johanna."

"Whatever, Casper."

"Miracles were not a priority for Sebastian, unless they suited his purpose. He didn't use his remarkable powers to ease the sorrows of others, or toward some greater good. The only thing that mattered to Sebastian was what he wanted, and he'd do whatever necessary to make something his own. He'd done terrible things to get what he wanted. And as you may know, bad deeds are like seeds, they begin quite small, but once planted they grow and grow, until they are so large, a small vessel cannot contain them. Sebastian's horrible actions had sewn seed upon seed, until his heart became a huge, dark forest, with barely room left for even the faintest bit of light. And like all those whose deeds are not suited to the sunlight's honesty, he traveled in secret, hidden within the shadows of night.

It was on one of these bitter evenings, a fierce storm blew in from the west. Heavy snow swirled and ice fell from the sky. Sebastian searched for shelter and found the very same cavern that our Gabriel had.

Sebastian entered the gloom and listened to the whistling sounds of the wind. Opening his gloved hand, he turned his palm face up and concentrated. In a low voice, he whispered, *"Thoghairm dóiteáin."* Blue fire flared up from his palm in a tall spire. Slowly it shrank, swirling down, until it sat neatly cradled in his hand. He held it out in front of him to light his way through the passage.

He continued on, until the cavern made the sharp turn and crossed the threshold into that same open area that Gabriel had found. Sebastian thought he saw a figure hiding in the shadows.

As he stepped closer, he called out "Who goes there? If you value your life, you'll reveal yourself at once!" Carefully, he inched forward, his hand bathing the ice maiden's face in sparkling, blue light.

There are moments that will change your mind, your heart, or even your destiny. In that one moment, everything changed for Sebastian. You'll hear people say that something "spoke to them," which doesn't mean that it actually uttered words, but instead that the thing in question made a connection with them. The ice maiden spoke to something hidden deep in a dusty corner of Sebastian's heart.

Staring at the ice maiden, Sebastian spoke in a voice both low and clear. "Greetings, my lady. I'm Sebastian the Sorcerer and it is an unexpected pleasure to make your acquaintance. Today is your lucky day. Magic is my trade, which means I can do *anything*. That includes bringing something as beautiful as you to life. And you, my dear, are too perfect not to be alive." Sebastian's mouth curved into an odd smile, the kind you might expect to see on a cat that's just found a mouse. "I'm going to make you real. Don't worry, it won't hurt. Well it most likely won't. But in any case, you'll

THE ICE MAIDEN'S TALE

be real and you'll be mine and you'll be far better off than you are right now."

Turning from her, Sebastian placed his heavy pack on the ground and heard it brush against something. Lowering his blue light, he saw the fiddle Gabriel had left behind. Pausing for a moment, he motioned with his empty hand, while his voice rang out, "*Dul!*" The bow and fiddle skidded across the floor and landed in the corner. Sebastian had far too much work to do to be bothered with useless things. And after all, what use could something as simple as a fiddle have for a powerful sorcerer?

You may be wondering how powerful Sebastian really was, and exactly how his magic worked. Deep desire for something and intense concentration were the ingredients for a successful spell. However, you must know that for everything a person takes in life there is a cost, and whether they are an ice maiden, a lonely artist or a powerful sorcerer, sooner or later they will have to pay the price.

The price Sebastian paid for his magic was that the larger the spell, the more energy it took from him. Spells of great magnitude would leave him so weak he could not move for as long as a day. And while it was a little thing to make blue fire in his hand, or move a small object, bringing the statue to life was a far more difficult task.

What will I need for this kind of spell, he wondered. *What will it take?* Sebastian thought of all the spells he'd done, both large and small and there was one—one spell that held a vivid place in his memory.

Three years before, when Sebastian was barely sixteen, he'd run away from home and stopped at an old fishing village along the Ambrian coast.

It was a clear night, and the sky was dotted with thousands of stars, sparkling against the blackness. The sound of waves rustling and the smell of salt and freshly caught fish filled the air. The crescent moon lit his way across the wooden pier and up the dirt road that wound through the cliffs, toward the village. Dotting the outcroppings of rock were small wooden shanties, some with lights on, others dark and silent. Away from these was a small chapel with a large copper bell in its tower. The church was quiet and empty, the perfect place for a runaway sorcerer to hide.

Sebastian climbed the stairs and opened the arched door. A small lantern at the front of the church cast a dim, honey-colored light over the pews. The floorboards creaked under his feet as he walked toward a locked door just to the side of the main room that led to the bell tower. Holding the door securely shut was a large iron lock.

With unblinking eyes, Sebastian stared at the rusty metal and whispered, *"Doras oscailte."* With those magic words, the lock slid off the door and fell into his waiting hands.

Closing the door behind him, he placed the lock in the pocket of his black cloak and climbed the stairs until he was standing on a grimy wooden platform, beneath the old church bell. Moonlight peered through the wooden slats around him and gave the room a ghostly air. Spider webs drooped from the overhead beams and the smell of dust and rain-soaked wood filled his nostrils. Lowering his pack, he settled himself for rest.

Sebastian stretched himself out on the floor. He shut his eyes, but a bone-chilling cold spread across him. Opening his eyes, he saw a faint shimmer in the corner, but it quickly disappeared. The platform had been empty when he'd arrived—he was sure of it, but now something sat across from him. Moving closer, he saw it was an old wooden chest covered with dust and dirt. *How could I have missed this?* Sebastian wondered. Running his hands over the lid and sides, he felt carvings encircling the box. In the darkness, he could not make out the inscription. Whispering, *"Thoghairm beag dóiteáin"*, he made a tiny blue flame rise from the palm of his hand. It was very small and gave off only the faintest light, exactly as Sebastian had wanted, since drawing attention to his hiding place would not be wise.

Bringing the light close, Sebastian examined the chest carefully. It appeared to be very old, its wood worn and cracked in some places, but its clasp sparkled a brilliant gold. Where did this come from? Sebastian wondered. How did something so valuable end up here?

Bending even closer he attempted to read the inscription. The carving was a series of large symbols in a language that seemed vaguely familiar, but still incomprehensible. Without hesitation, he opened the box.

On a frayed, water-stained pillow sat a gold medallion on a long cord. The round disk seemed almost to glow against the darkness. Resembling an old coin, it was engraved with a symbol that Sebastian had never seen before. Reaching out, his fingers touched the metal.

His skin began to tingle, as if little spiders were crawling up his arms and legs. A sudden wind blew through the bell tower and shook the rafters. Sebastian's hand closed tightly over the medallion and snatched it up.

The wind grew strong, so strong in fact that it caused the heavy old bell to ring out, piercing the stillness; the sound, dreadfully loud. Sebastian grabbed his pack, ran down the stairs, through the church, and toward the shore. The clanging of the bell continued, the sound more anxious the farther away Sebastian ran. His heart knocked harder and harder against his ribs, as he searched frantically for a way to escape.

As though out of thin air, men materialized from the shanties, their lanterns bobbing through the darkness. Sebastian made it as far as the docks, where he was trapped by a large group of angry fisherman. They closed in around him, forcing him back and toward the shore. Sebastian clutched the medallion tightly, while his mind searched for a spell, for something, anything that would help him.

In the distance the old bell kept tolling, and as the men grew even closer, fear rushed through Sebastian. He couldn't concentrate on a single spell. All his thoughts were pulled to the medallion that pulsed hot against his chest. So, he focused all his power on it and cast a simple spell. Sebastian's voice rang out, summoning help. "Thoghairm cabhair," he cried. Lightning crashed across the sky and a huge wave began to form. The fisherman stood like statues, stunned by the spectacle, unable to run from the danger. Sebastian took his opportunity and backed away from the mesmerized villagers, quickly moving up the slope behind him. With an enormous crash, the wave pounded upon the men, the edge of it barely touching Sebastian's boot.

The clanging of the bell stopped and the water receded. There was not a single fisherman left, no trace that any men had once stood there--not a hat, or a boot, or even a solitary shoelace. Words are powerful things. Sebastian had asked for help, but had never specified the exact kind.

What have I done? Sebastian thought as he stared down at the medallion in his trembling hands and then again at the ocean. A feeling spread through his belly, like he'd eaten something terrible, and could not lose the taste of it. Suddenly Sebastian was weak and dizzy. Behind him on the edge of the slope was a small rowboat waiting for its master, one who'd most likely been tossed into the sea.

With the last of his dwindling strength, Sebastian pushed it out into the water and collapsed inside. He lay asleep, cradled in the boat, without strength left even to dream.

The waves softly lapped against the little boat and quietly carried him away from the bell tower and the shanties and the empty docks where the fishermen had taken their last look upon the world.

In the ice maiden's cave, Sebastian grasped the medallion that hung around his neck, remembering the look on the faces of the men as they'd been swept out to sea. Their expressions had been filled with both horror and awe. Although the fierce sorcerer would never admit it, part of him was sickened by the memory. And even now, Sebastian still dreamt of those shouting voices and the churning water.

As night grew into morning and morning into night, Sebastian huddled in front of the statue, whispering enchantment after enchantment, but none succeeded. He went without sleep for days and ate only small bites of the dried fruit and meat he carried with him in his pack. His eyes were bloodshot and his body ached from lack of sleep, but still he continued. No matter how complicated the incantation or how much he concentrated, his spells just wouldn't work.

It was then that the Sebastian discovered a vital truth: It is a far greater task to create life than to destroy it.

2

FAILURE & FRIENDSHIP

"Sebastian rocks!" said Casper.

"Why, because he killed a bunch of poor fishermen?" Johanna replied disgustedly.

"No! Because he could do it so easily. Besides, they were chasing him so he had to do it. He was just protecting himself!"

"That's not true. He had other options. If he's so good with magic he could have done something else."

"He freaked out, Johanna. He thought they'd kill him or something."

"It doesn't matter. He killed all those men and that just makes him a villain."

"Villains can be cool. Just look at Lex Luthor or the Joker."

"I bet if you were one of those fishermen you wouldn't think Sebastian's cool!"

"I'd be dead so I couldn't think anything!" Casper countered.

"Being dead isn't something to joke about!"

"Children," Mrs. Kinder interrupted. "It's not necessary to debate Sebastian's coolness just yet. Besides, aren't you forgetting about someone?"

"Gabriel! Yes, let's go back to him. He's *much* cooler than Sebastian," Johanna said.

"Yeah right. All that music and art, he's so much of a wuss, he's basically a girl."

"How many times have I told you that girls are not wusses, and if you keep talking like that, one day a girl who's bigger than you is going to give you a black eye. If Mom wouldn't ground me for it, I'd do it myself."

"I'd like to see you try!" Casper laughed.

"You're so ridiculous; it's pointless to argue with you." Johanna answered.

"Good. Then we're all in agreement that the arguing is over and the story can start up again," said Mrs. Kinder. "Now let's get back to our wandering artist. After leaving his beloved ice maiden in the Frozen

Forest, Gabriel journeyed down many paths, over a mountain and across a river, into the land where the lemon trees grow."

* * * *

As Gabriel followed the cobblestone road that wound and wound its way toward the village, his eyes searched the horizon. They rested on the oceans of green trees filled with cheerful yellow lemons stretching out as far as he could see. Not a single tree was cold or frozen. Swaying gracefully back and forth in the breeze, all the trees in the lemon forest danced in time.

Hugging his small leather satchel to his chest, Gabriel continued up the path. As the sun set, the moon rose to cast a lovely spell over the lemon trees, changing their yellow fruit to silver. All around fireflies began their nightly rounds, flittering through the trees, and lighting the way to the little lemon village.

The beauty of this new place brought Gabriel little comfort. The ache he had felt when leaving the ice maiden had not lessened. He couldn't see the brilliance of the moon, or the serene beauty of the trees, or even the wonder of the sparkling fireflies. The image of the maiden had imprinted itself in his mind. And with each step he took toward the village, he saw her face with its sad eyes and wondered to himself, "Does she miss my music?"

As the early morning sun began to peer out over the treetops, Gabriel entered the village. The streets were narrow and lined with small buildings. Each had colorful plants and painted signs out front.

There was a pink one for the bakery, where lemon tarts, lemon meringue pies, and lemon custard cakes peeked out appetizingly through the windows. An orange sign swung from a pole next to the library, where benches and hibiscus flowers lined the front walk. Down the street a little farther, past some white shuttered houses, there was a sign for the town inn. Faded blue letters spelled out the place where travelers went for supper and a comfortable bed. And so, Gabriel made his way past the quiet shops and the shuttered windows to grasp the ring at the inn's front door.

He pushed open the door and was greeted by the innkeeper. Her long, gray hair fell in two braids, each tied at the end with a gold ribbon. Sparkling in the morning sunlight, beaded necklaces and bracelets covered her neck and wrists. She greeted him with a smile.

"Welcome, traveler. You must be hungry and tired. We have the perfect room for you. It's just up the winding stairs at the top of our clock tower. It has the best view of the village, if I do say so myself. Meals are served in the tavern, just through that door." She motioned, making her bracelets and necklaces jingle like a music box. "How long will you be staying with us?"

Gabriel was taken aback for a moment at the Innkeeper's cheerful and rapidly spoken introduction. "I'm not entirely sure," answered Gabriel. "I'm passing through town, but if I can find some work I may stay a bit longer."

"What kind of work do you do?" asked the Innkeeper.

"A little of this and that--but mostly I'm a sculptor."

"So, you make statues?"

"Sometimes," answered Gabriel, a hint of sadness in his voice.

"Then you're in luck. The library has wanted a statue for years. They've never been able to find someone who knew how to carve. We have lots of painters in town, but no one who can make statutes. I bet if you went down there, they'd give you the job."

"Thank you for your kindness." Gabriel handed the innkeeper three small, gold coins to pay for the cost of his room for a week. She walked him over to the staircase and pointed toward his room. Placing his satchel over his shoulder, he made his way up the wooden staircase that spiraled through the tower.

Sebastian was still hard at work inside the cavern. He had stopped his incantations and moved on to mixing potions with ingredients like bat wings, wolf fangs and boysenberries, then pouring them around the statue. All his endeavors accomplished were to change the color of the ice on the floor around the lady. First it turned a lovely red, then an unfortunate green, next a shade of pink almost the exact color of a watermelon's insides, and finally back to clear ice.

Each unsuccessful attempt made Sebastian angrier. It was as though a storm cloud were hanging over him and growing larger with each of his failures. He had never wanted a spell to work more and no spell had ever given him this much difficulty.

"Why do you taunt me!" he screamed at the ice maiden. "You should be alive by now! Why won't you obey?"

With that outburst Sebastian grabbed his cloak and left the cave. Outside the entrance, he paced anxiously back and forth, his thoughts spinning. Sebastian analyzed the ingredients to a hundred different potions and reviewed the words to countless incantations and came to the realization that he'd already tried everything that had even a slight chance of success. *What is there left to do* he thought. *What else can I possibly try?*

Sebastian needed to know exactly what it would take to bring a stubborn ice maiden to life. He had exhausted his magical arsenal and needed help. There was one place where he thought he could find it.

But before Sebastian began that journey, he needed a place to rest and gather supplies. Remembering a little cabin he'd seen, he headed in that direction.

Through the dense snow, Sebastian trudged down the steep, icy slope leading away from the cave. As the freezing wind blew at his cheeks, he paused for a moment and wondered if the ice maiden would be safe alone. He shrugged off his worries. *If anyone tries to take her, I'll make them pay.*

Sebastian arrived at the front door of the cabin. The dwelling reminded him of a place he'd been before, there was a strange familiarity to the wooden door and sloped chimney. Silently, he checked to see if anyone was home. There was no light in the house; no smoke coming from the chimney. The cabin was empty.

Sebastian stared at the door, concentrating all his energy and whispered "*Oscail doras.*" The padlock fell off, and with a small whine, the door opened. He walked across the threshold into Gabriel's humble cottage.

The first thing he noticed was the wooden workman's table. On both sides of it were shelves filled with chisels and hammers of all different sizes, lined up in neat rows. Sitting in front of the stone fireplace, with a bearskin rug beneath it, was an empty rocking chair. It seemed to ask for a warm body to fill it again.

Sebastian shut the cabin door behind him and, though he had not been invited, made himself at home. He started a fire in the fireplace, took jars of food from the cupboard, and even napped on the small, warm bed. When he felt refreshed and ready to leave, he pawed through the tools on the shelves above the workbench, looking for something of interest.

One thing struck Sebastian immediately--a large chisel whose carved handle was smooth and lined with swirls of different colored wood. It was, if you remember, one of Gabriel's prized possessions and the very same chisel with which he carved the ice maiden.

After Gabriel had left the cave, he'd been afraid to take the chisel, fearing that the memories of the ice maiden were somehow carved into the edges of it. Although it broke his heart, he left it behind in his cabin and took other tools instead.

Sebastian of course, didn't know the origin of the chisel, didn't know the important role it had played in the creation of his obsession. All he knew was that something about it interested him. And as was his habit with trinkets that caught his eye, he slipped the chisel into his cloak pocket, and grabbing his heavy pack, passed through the doorway and into the cold.

Gabriel walked through the village, passing farmers in straw hats driving horse carts full of gleaming lemons. He continued along, until he came to the library. Two stories high and built of large polished stones, it was surrounded by red flowers that smelled faintly of cinnamon.

He followed a path of golden stepping stones and entered a garden just off the side of the building. In the center of a circle of benches, was a huge block of yellow stone. Flecked with veins of gold, it sparkled in the sunlight. Moving closer, Gabriel ran his palms over its smooth surface.

"May I help you?" asked a voice stiffly. Gabriel turned to greet a spindly man wearing wire-rimmed glasses and a petulant expression.

"I'm looking for the Librarian."

Peering over his glasses, he gave Gabriel a long look. "Your search is over. I am the one and only. How may I be of assistance?"

"The innkeeper mentioned you were looking for someone to carve a statue for your library."

"Yes, of course we are!" the Librarian exclaimed in a surprisingly excited manner, his voice quickening. "It seems as though we've been looking forever for someone who can do the job. You see some years back a generous benefactor donated that lovely block of stone behind you to the library for the specific purpose of creating a statue. But so far no one's been able to do it. Of course we've had many people come through here and *talk* about all the marvelous things they'd create—they've all just been swindlers of some kind or another." He paused for a moment, considering what he'd said. "Do you have any sort of references I could check?"

Gabriel rummaged into his satchel and pulled out a small, wooden bird. It was delicate and intricately carved. It seemed so lifelike that one expected it to suddenly start twittering. The librarian took the bird from Gabriel, eyeing it carefully.

"So you think you can handle this job?" asked the librarian, handing the bird back.

Placing the carving back in his satchel, Gabriel replied, "I'm a sculptor by trade and although I've never seen stone quite like what you've got here, I'm sure I can make something suitable. What kind of object did you have in mind?"

"That's the second problem, we don't know!"

"In all this time you haven't chosen something?"

Drawing himself up, the Librarian said haughtily, "Well there's been a lot of debate. Besides, it's not as though we've ever had someone who could do the job."

"What were some of the suggestions?"

"A giant lemon seemed to be a popular sentiment, sort of a tribute to the town, if you will."

"There seem to be a lot of lemons around here already." Gabriel responded.

The Librarian puffed up almost like a peacock. "Well, I didn't say it was *unique*, I said it was a *tribute*. Do *you* have a better suggestion?"

"I'm not sure. I'll need some time to think about it."

"Of course you will. And I'm quite sure *you'll* be able to come up with something when *no one else* has."

Gabriel looked thoughtfully at the stone. "It wants to be something. The trick is to figure out what."

"Yes, of course," responded the Librarian in a sarcastic tone. "The pay is sixty gold coins, thirty when you start and the remaining thirty when the job is completed. We also supply your midday meal."

"That sounds more than fair."

"All right then…ah, well, ah I'll just ah…let you…get started."

"Thank you." Sitting on one of the benches, Gabriel stared at the stone. The Librarian shook his head, shrugged his shoulders, and went inside. Long after the sun had set and the fireflies came out to dance, Gabriel was still sitting.

"Ah-hem," coughed the Librarian. Gabriel didn't move. "Excuse me," the Librarian continued.

"Yes," Gabriel replied, breaking out of his reverie.

"I'm closing up, you can stop..uh..*working...*" Reluctantly, the Librarian pulled out a small velvet bag from his waistcoat pocket. "As per our agreement, here are your thirty gold coins."

Opening the velvet bag, Gabriel removed ten gold coins and handed the bag back to the Librarian.

"When I start chiseling, you can give me the rest."

Visibly relieved, the Librarian responded quickly, "Very well then, I'll see you first thing tomorrow morning," he paused for a moment then continued, "and I do mean *first* thing—no dawdling." The Librarian turned and with even more haste left the garden. Gabriel paid him little attention and kept sitting, as still as a statue.

Every day for five straight days Gabriel sat staring at the stone. Sometimes he'd take out his leather bound sketchbook and charcoal pencil as though he were going to begin a drawing. But always its pages remained dishearteningly blank.

The ache Gabriel felt so keenly when he'd first entered the village intensified with each passing day. No matter how hard he tried to focus on the project and the golden stone, all that filled his mind was the ice maiden. Alongside the sadness growing inside him, fear began to sprout.

He'd sit in the library garden and ask himself, "What if I start chiseling away and my angel appears? What if she returns? How can I let her go again?" In his mind the words echoed, "*I can't. I can't. I can't.*"

Each day while Gabriel went through this agonizing ritual, the Librarian brought him his lunch. Placing the tray on the bench next to Gabriel, the Librarian muttered phrases like, "He's absolutely mad—he even talks to himself," and "What kind of Sculptor doesn't even lift up a chisel" and "It's obvious you can't do it, just give up already." In Gabriel's heart fear pounded out those familiar words, "*You can't. You can't. You can't.*"

All the while Gabriel struggled; villagers would stop to watch him. With each passing day more and more would crowd around. "Swindler!" "Crook!" "Phony!" — some loud folks would yell. But most would just murmur, point, and laugh.

On the seventh day, Gabriel marched up to the stone. Moving close, he took a deep breath and raised his hammer and pick. He pulled back his hand to strike the stone and the crowd of onlookers gave a collective gasp. Just as he was going to hit the stone, his arms began to shake, and he dropped his pick. A voice from the crowd called out, "Fraud!" and one rather foul fellow threw a rotten lemon at him. It took no time at all for them to clear out of the library garden, their exclamations of disgust and disbelief trailing through the air.

Gabriel's thoughts were dark and painful. Maybe the Librarian was right—maybe he couldn't make their statue. Maybe he couldn't sculpt anymore. Maybe he'd never make another statue as long as he lived! Maybe the ice maiden was the last thing he was ever going to create! Those thoughts left him feeling hollow and unhappier than when he'd first left her cave.

Under the waning moon and the amber streetlights, he left the library and made his way to the tavern which adjoined the inn. Brimming with townspeople dining together, the room was filled with the smell of warm bread and roasted meat. The sound of clunking glasses resounded through the space. Wooden tables surrounded by battered stools held dripping beeswax candles, and in the far corner of the room, flames danced in a large stone fireplace. It was crowded. There was not a single empty table to be found and not a single welcoming face.

Gabriel turned to leave when suddenly a woman's voice called out. "Stranger, there's room at my table. Come join me." He turned, scanning the room until his eyes rested on a lone woman at a table nestled in the corner near the fireplace.

Her skin was the color of olives dipped in honey and her long dark hair was interwoven with bright peacock feathers. Layer upon layer of copper and gold jewelry adorned her neck, arms, and hands. As Gabriel approached her, he was struck by her eyes. Matching the feathers in her hair, one eye was a deep blue, the other a startling green. And although she seemed the same age as him, her eyes seemed lifetimes older.

She gave him a slow smile and motioned for him to join her. Pulling out the wooden stool across from her, he sat down.

"You're not from around here," she said.

"No, I'm not," answered Gabriel, wondering what this strange girl wanted from him.

"Neither am I," she answered. "I'm a Gypsy and I can always spot a fellow traveler." She winked at him. "You must be the infamous sculptor who's supposed to make a statue for the library. I'm sure you must know by now that you've given the village an entirely new sport."

"Sport?"

"Yes, they appear to have made gossiping about you a pastime," she responded with a laugh.

"I didn't realize I was of so much interest to the villagers," replied Gabriel defensively.

"You're a stranger here and strangers are always interesting."

"Is that why you called me over here, because I seem interesting?"

"No," A hint of sadness sparkled in her eyes, "you seem as though you could use a friend."

Gabriel paused for a moment, and wondered how long it had been since he had a friend. The image of the ice maiden flickered in his mind. "You may be right, but what about you? What do you get out of be-friending a strange sculptor?"

She gave him another smile, the kind that usually precedes a secret, and answered, "Maybe I could use a friend as well."

"Then it seems quite fortunate that we met." Gabriel responded with a smile.

"Yes," she answered, "Yes, it does."

"I'm Gabriel and you are?"

"People call me the Gypsy."

"That's your name?"

She let out another laugh. "I didn't say that was my name, that's just what people call me."

"It's an odd sort of friendship, where you won't even tell me your name?"

A serious look crossed her lovely eyes for a moment. "Gabriel, there is only one other person in the whole world who knows my name. Perhaps someday, I shall make it two—but for now that's all I will say."

A serving maid appeared asking what they'd like for supper. She returned shortly carrying two large plates of roasted lamb with spiced turnips and two mugs of yellow ale. They sat eating their dinner and chatting.

"So what is it that you do?" Gabriel asked after swallowing a bite of the fragrant lamb.

"I read tea leaves and on occasion, palms."

"So you tell people their fortunes?"

"Sometimes," she answered. "And sometimes I tell them their past. And there are some things you don't need tea leaves to see."

"Such as?"

"Sorrow," the Gypsy answered. "There is sadness in your eyes, and something more." She watched him carefully, "Something in your past holds you very tightly." Gabriel had not expected her response and struggled to keep surprise from showing on his face. The Gypsy paused for a moment, took a sip from her mug, and continued, "Then of course there is the matter of your work at the library."

"What about it?"

"The rumors suggest that you haven't actually done any work. Having walked by the Library and seen a big block of stone instead of a statue, it appears to me that the rumors may be true."

"You don't understand," Gabriel answered weakly. Hunched over the table, he looked like a balloon after its air had run out. "I can't do it."

"Why not? Don't you know how?"

"Yes, of course I do, but I don't know what to make, but that's not really all of it..." he paused, and then added, "there's more."

"There's always more," she nodded and touched his arm. The warmth of her fingers felt reassuring to Gabriel. How long had it been since he'd felt a warm touch? "You'll find I'm as good at listening as I am at telling fortunes, so why don't you tell me what's troubling you?"

Hope fluttered inside Gabriel's chest. He didn't know why, but something inside him said he could trust the Gypsy—that she really was his friend and maybe, just maybe, he could tell her some things he hadn't told anyone else.

"It started one night when I found a cave—there was this block of ice. And I saw, well I thought I saw someone inside it—it's crazy I know." His story poured out of him like rocks tumbling down a mountainside. He told the Gypsy about his creation of the ice maiden and how she haunted him. He spoke of his fiddle and how he'd left it behind with the statue, and even about the Librarian's taunts. Gabriel talked and talked and talked—more than he ever had before.

All the while the Gypsy sat quietly listening to his desperation. She watched him, eyes brimming with understanding, and when Gabriel finally ended his story, the tavern was nearly empty. The only sound left in the room was the steady drip of water from a barrel on a high shelf.

She squeezed his hand and he spoke again, "I can't, I just can't."

"You must," she answered. "There will always be someone to tell you that you can't do something. On occasion it will be for your own good, but other times it will simply be out of fear. That silly Librarian is just afraid—afraid of what it will mean if you do succeed."

"But I don't even know where to start," Gabriel answered with a sigh.

"At the beginning, of course."

"How silly of me. I thought I'd start at the end."

The Gypsy laughed, "You're making jokes, so that's already a sign that the tides are turning."

"I still don't understand what you mean about the beginning."

"You will." She smiled and gave his hand another squeeze. "I have faith in you, so have a little faith in yourself."

He walked the Gypsy to her room, her long skirt rustling down the narrow hallway. Standing by the door, Gabriel clasped her hand in his, and said gently, "Your kindness has meant so much to me. Someday, I'll find a way to repay you. I promise."

"There are never debts among friends," she answered giving him a smile so charming, Gabriel felt his heart jump a little in his chest. "Now get a good night's rest—you have plenty of work ahead of you tomorrow."

"Yes, I do. Goodnight," he answered. Jewelry jingling, she stepped inside her room and shut the door. Gabriel climbed softly up the stairs, feeling just a little lighter. With each step he wondered what his new and mysterious friend had meant about starting at the beginning.

"So, did Gabriel fall in love with the Gypsy?" asked Johanna, her voice a bit more wistful than she intended.

"Love's a complicated thing. For now, let's keep it simple and say that Gabriel and the Gypsy stumbled into a deep friendship." Mrs. Kinder responded.

"Friendship," Johanna whined, sounding oddly like Casper. "Friendship is boring," she finished with a sigh.

"Talk like that would make someone think you'd never really had a friend! Friendships are very special, one of the most special things in all the world, they have their own sort of magic. When you're lost and alone and feel like there's nothing left in the world, friendship can rescue you--"

"This is BORing!" interrupted Casper. "Enough with all this girlie *love* stuff. I want to get back to the Sorcerer—Sebastian—is he doing any other spells—did he kill anyone else—"

"—Casper, the whole story is not about magic and killing people," interrupted Johanna.

"How do you know—it's not *your* story."

A loud rapping echoed through the house, making Johanna jump a bit.

"It sounds like someone is at the door." Mrs. Kinder rose to answer it. She returned with Casper and Johanna's mother.

Johanna always thought of her mom as medium: medium height, medium brown hair, and medium good looks, except for her eyes and her laugh. Those were special. Every time Johanna's mother would laugh, her vivid green eyes would crinkle around the edges. And that laugh, it was *perfect*. Bright and sweet, whenever her mother laughed, Johanna couldn't help but join in. Unfortunately, it had been some time since either Johanna or Casper had seen her laugh, and lately her eyes had been lined with dark circles.

"Thank you so much Mrs. Kinder for watching the children."

"It was my pleasure, Emily. We had a lovely day. And I'm happy to watch them any time."

"Would you be able to watch them again tomorrow night? I'm going to have to stay at the hospital late because of the surgery."

Surgery? Johanna thought, and gave Casper a nervous look. His eyes instinctively narrowed.

"It will probably be past dinnertime. I can leave you some money to order pizza—" Emily continued.

"Oh pish-posh. I'll make a lovely supper and the children can help me. It will be fun, right kids?"

"Uh," Johanna stuttered, while Casper just let out a sigh and crossed his arms. Seeing the desperate expression on her mother's face, Johanna quickly answered, "Yes, we'll have a lot of fun. It will be great."

Emily Sullivan's expression relaxed a bit. "Thanks so much Mrs. Kinder, I can't tell you how much I appreciate it."

"It does an old lady good to be around kids, and neighbors need to look out for one another."

"Kids, go get your coats and let's get home." Johanna and Casper ran to the coat stand, and Johanna couldn't shake the knot in her stomach that had formed at the word *surgery*. It sounded so big and serious and dangerous. *Would it hurt Dad?* She wondered. It must, since cuts hurt, but they put you to sleep so you don't really know you're being cut. So maybe it really isn't so bad?

They returned to their mother and tugged on their coats.

"I'll have them come by right after the school bus drops them off. Don't worry about them doing homework, it can wait 'til the weekend."

"Wonderful. We'll have plenty of time to finish our story and make supper," Mrs. Kinder answered.

"Wonderful," grumbled Casper to himself.

"Now kids, thank Mrs. Kinder and we'll be on our way."

"Thank you," the children replied in unison. Although Johanna's voice was a bit hollow and Casper's somewhat exasperated.

"Thank you again, Mrs. Kinder. You have all my numbers in case there are any problems."

Mrs. Sullivan and her children left the house and went down the droopy steps. Mrs. Kinder watched from the doorway as Casper ran across the street to the Sullivan's quaint blue house while Johanna and their mother followed.

"Mom, can I see Dad before the surgery?" Johanna asked.

"I'm sorry honey, your Dad really can't have any visitors. He needs to be in isolation. As soon as he's doing better, you and Casper can see him."

"Is he going to get better?" Johanna asked, a heaviness settling in her heart.

"Hurry up!" Casper called out. "I'm hungry!"

"Calm down, Casper! We're almost there." Mrs. Sullivan yelled. She put her arm around Johanna's shoulder and gave a little squeeze. They hurried up the stairs to the white trimmed house and unlocked the door. Casper ran inside, threw himself down on the dark green living room couch and turned on the TV.

Emily looked tired and put her keys and purse down on the living room table, then took off her coat and slipped out of her shoes. She reminded Johanna of a sleepwalker. "Kids, I was thinking some Chinese tonight. Is the usual okay?"

"Just remember my noodles!" Casper chimed in.

"That's fine," Johanna answered.

When the food came, the three members of the Sullivan household sat at the kitchen table, each ignoring the fourth empty chair. It drove Johanna crazy that Casper only ever ate sesame noodles and the crunchy noodles that you could dip into duck sauce (although he refused to eat duck sauce—stating adamantly that sauces made from ducks were disgusting). Johanna liked to try different things, but dumplings were her favorite. She'd let her parents choose the kind that way she'd be surprised when she bit into one. But tonight, she didn't care what they ordered. Her stomach ached and she couldn't help but miss her Dad. He always used to read the fortune cookies in funny voices and was the only one who liked the spicy shrimp. Tonight their mother hadn't even ordered it. Did that mean he'd never come back? That they'd never need to order spicy shrimp again?

"Johanna, you haven't touched your food. Are you all right?" Emily Sullivan looked at her daughter and worried. While she knew Casper didn't really understand the seriousness of things, Johanna was different.

"I'm just not hungry tonight. May I be excused?"

"All right, just go shower before bed." As Johanna turned to go up the stairs, "Wait, honey don't you want a fortune cookie?" Emily asked as she held up the plastic wrapped treat.

"That's okay." Johanna answered and continued up the stairs. Johanna took a quick shower and went into her bedroom. It housed a large oak bookshelf with more books crammed in it then could comfortably fit, a small tidy desk that matched the bookshelf, and a tall dresser. Topping the dresser was a jewelry box carved with wooden roses that had belonged to her great grandmother Liesel, and was where Johanna kept her favorite treasures.

Johanna sat down on her bed, and stared at her quilt, running her fingers along the pattern. She'd bought it six months back, before her father had gotten sick. She hadn't wanted anything too flowery or silly, and had been explicit in requesting something "grown up," so her Dad took her to the department store and let her look around. She chose one with simple green and brown stripes. Her Dad had said, "Joey, don't you think that's a little boring for you? Grown up, doesn't mean boring, you know." He'd said it with a smile. He helped her search until they found the perfect pattern of green ivy on a white background. After they were done shopping, they'd stopped at the ice cream parlor and shared a banana split. "Don't tell Casper or your Mom. It'll be our secret celebration for successful shopping."

Johanna's father had never been one of those Dads who refused to do things because they were "girl stuff". He was just as content to spend an hour looking at bedspreads with Johanna as playing catch with Casper. She'd had so many fun times with her father; she couldn't imagine a world without him. And most of all she didn't want to imagine it.

Johanna lay down on the quilt and pulled a fisted hand up to her heart, as if that alone would keep it from spilling out.

The next day Johanna and Casper once again went up the sagging steps to Mrs. Kinder's house.

"Do you think Dad's okay?" Casper asked, breaking the silence between brother and sister.

"I'm sure he'll be fine. He has really good doctors and Mom is there with him." Johanna wished she believed those words. But she knew if Casper had asked her, it meant he was worried. She wondered if his stomach felt like it was eating itself. And if his heart felt hollow, like the Easter bunnies that are only thin chocolate shell, instead of being solid inside.

"I wonder if she'll finally kill us today." Casper said.

"She's just a harmless old lady, so be good. She's only been nice to us until now."

"But that's what all the smart witches do. They're nice and they butter you up until they want to throw you in the pot for supper. And tonight, she's cooking! Kids: the other white meat," Casper gulped.

Johanna let out a sigh, "Enough already." She turned away from Casper, grabbed the knocker and rapped it quickly.

Almost immediately, the door opened and there stood Mrs. Kinder in a blue flowered dress and a yellow apron.

"Well there you are, dearies. Come on in, it's cold outside—head right into the sitting room and I'll get you both something warm to drink."

When Mrs. Kinder's back was turned, Casper mouthed the word *poison*. Johanna just rolled her eyes in response.

The two children went into the sitting room and took off their coats. Mrs. Kinder returned with a tray of three mugs.

"These are my extra special cocoa recipe. My late husband just adored it."

Casper whipped his head around and gave Johanna a glaring look, clearly indicating that he was sure the "special recipe" was poison, and if they died it would be all Johanna's fault.

Mrs. Kinder handed them each a mug, and said, "Now let's get on with the story."

"Wait. Don't you need the book?" Johanna asked.

"Yes, of course." Mrs. Kinder replied quickly. "How silly of me. I swear my brain is getting addled. You live too long and you start to forget things." Mrs. Kinder went over to the bookcase, and again Johanna couldn't see her grab the book, but when she turned around it was in her hands. "It looks like it's time us to turn our eyes and ears back to our wayward Sorcerer."

Mrs. Kinder adjusted her glasses, cleared her throat, and continued. Her voice was lower than usual and a bit solemn.

"Many different paths will take you to the same place. The Sorcerer had two choices that would get him to his destination. Clearly marked, one path circled the forest and was the choice of most travelers. The other was shadowy and cold, and wound right through the dangerous woods—not a journey many souls would wish to take. But Sebastian was no ordinary traveler, so you can guess which path he chose."

3

PATHS & CHOICES

Sebastian stepped into the Frozen Forest, his boots crunching the dead branches that covered the ground. The night was terribly dark, clouds hid the stars, and even the moon refused to show her face. An icy, gray mist snaked through the trees. Stretching toward the sky, the trees' branches looked like skeletal hands reaching out from old graves.

Walking for hours, Sebastian continued through the woods. A stinging wind blew, making an unearthly whistling sound as it struck the frozen limbs of the forest. Pulling his heavy cloak around him, Sebastian struggled to keep from shivering. *It's near here*, he thought, *just a bit farther. I know he's close by.*

Up ahead was a large hill of jagged rocks and small, dark openings. Shutting his eyes, Sebastian called out in a sharp voice, "*Thoghairm Coimeádaí!*" and a bolt of purple lightning cracked.

A booming voice rang out, "Who dares to awaken me?" It echoed from the rock crevices and made the entire hill tremble. "Whosoever seeks me out shall find only death!" Rocks began to slide down rapidly, and the branches crackled, reaching out toward Sebastian.

"Goblin! I know your tricks! Show yourself at once! I've no time for your nonsense!" Impatiently, Sebastian waved his arm, yelling "*Stad!*" Abruptly the trees' limbs moved back into place and the trembling stopped. A purple mist swirled in a miniature cyclone and with a great *swoosh* a small goblin appeared before him.

The Goblin dusted his hands on his patchwork pants and adjusted his small, red cap over his pointed ears. His pale green skin glowed brightly in the darkness. A long chain of tarnished metal hung over his shoulder and continued down across his chest. Dangling from each link were odd items: a fishing lure, a rusted spoon, a dented thimble, and even a silver key.

His beady eyes gleaming a midnight blue, the Goblin said, "Raag, ye still's impatient as ever. With all that power ye tink ye'd learn to 'joy a lil mischief from time ta time."

"My time is too valuable to waste on games."

The Goblin tilted his head and gave Sebastian a wondering look. "Klaarg, what's life if not a game?" When Sebastian gave no answer, the Goblin waved his hand and went on: "Raag, no matter! I've learnt by now not ta reason with ye whent yer in the middle of one of yer quests. Klaarg, what do ye need this time? Sumthin fer a paralyzing spell? A new poison? Ye fightin anotha giant?"

"No, no. I'm through with giants and I don't need any poison. I'm looking for a different kind of potion. So far, none of my formulas have worked." Sebastian's voice took on a note of urgency, "I need something larger—more powerful."

The Goblin's curiosity was piqued. "Raag! Klaarg, what inna world is more powerful than takin' life?"

"Giving it," answered Sebastian.

The Goblin was startled by the response and paused for a moment before he spoke. "Klaarg, why would ye want ta do that? What's in it fer ye?"

"That's none of your concern. I need to find the right magic to bring something that's not alive to life."

The Goblin nodded, as though finally understanding. "Klaarg, ye mean ye want ta raise the dead?"

"No, I want to make something alive that's *never* been alive," replied Sebastian emphatically.

The Goblin began running his long, gnarled fingers along his heavy chain, making its ornaments clunk together. "Raag, that s'plains why ye've had trouble."

"What do you mean?" Sebastian demanded.

"Raag--that isna yer kind of magic."

"What! That's impossible! It's *all* my kind of magic!"

"Raag! What ye ask will be nearly impossible fer ye ta do!"

"Nearly impossible is not the same as impossible."

"Raag. No," answered the Goblin carefully. "That will depend 'tirely upon ye. Ye have a tiny chance at succeedin."

"Tell me what I need to do! Which ingredients? What spells?"

"Raag, this is not somethin I canna help ye with. I'm jus a keeper of lost an forgotten things, this isnna my kinda magic either." The purple cyclone swirled around the Goblin again and in a moment, he was gone.

"*Mallachtaí!*" Sebastian bellowed, and a huge rift opened up in the forest floor in response to his anger. "How dare you refuse to help me!" Sebastian screamed. "All that nonsense about it not being my kind of magic—all magic is my magic!" he screamed, his voice echoing throughout the Frozen Forest. If you won't help me, there are others far more powerful who will!

Yes, thought Sebastian, *I know exactly where to go next.*

Back at the lemon village, Gabriel awoke with the Gypsy's words echoing through his head. He dressed, ate a quick breakfast at the tavern, and walked toward the library, wondering over and over what it meant to "*begin at the beginning.*"

"She believes in me," he said to himself. "I must succeed." Instead of sitting and staring as usual, Gabriel turned and walked away from the library, down the cobblestone road that led into the heart of the village.

Past shops and houses, Gabriel arrived at the market square. In the center of the open space was a large tiered fountain that cascaded water flecked with gold. Surrounding it were countless peddlers selling all manner of items from their small carts and stalls. The sounds of people haggling and goods being weighted, wrapped and loaded into bags and baskets made the market a noisy, but cheerful place.

Gabriel observed the peddlers with deep fascination: the farmer wearing a blue bandana who sold onions and turnips, the young lady with long blonde hair touting colorful crystal necklaces as "guaranteed love charms," and an old woman laughing with a young girl as they knit blankets with bright designs.

The knitters fascinated Gabriel, so he moved closer to them. He watched as the old woman's wrinkled fingers closed over the girl's smaller ones, and how with tenderness she guided them over the colorful yarn. She was a patient teacher and reminded Gabriel of his grandfather.

Gabriel's grandfather had been a woodcarver and on cold winter evenings he'd sit in his rocking chair, smoking his pipe and carving. His grandfather never spoke, and whether he was unable or simply unwilling Gabriel never knew. But his grandfather's love for him was so obvious it never needed words. His grandfather cooked all his meals, washed and darned his clothes, and tucked him into bed each and every night. He taught Gabriel how to navigate through the woods, how to find food and most importantly how to carve.

His grandfather would sit next to the little boy and with great patience demonstrate how to cut into the wood. Gabriel, frustrated at his inability, would toss the wood block to the ground. Every time this happened, his grandfather would bend down, pick it up and place it gently back into Gabriel's hands. Laying a warm hand on Gabriel's shoulder, he'd give him a small pat, and start the lesson again. Lesson after lesson continued this way, and when Gabriel nicked himself with his knife, his grandfather would bandage him up and they'd begin just where they'd left off.

The first things Gabriel learned to carve were roses. Over time they changed from odd bumps to perfectly formed blossoms. Carrying bunches of carved wooden roses, he and his grandfather would make a trip to the nearby town of Edystone. Walking through its gates and down a stone path, they'd enter a quiet cemetery and stop at three gravestones near the corner fence and leave their roses.

Every time Gabriel visited the cemetery, he'd stare at the carved names of his parents and grandmother and search his mind for a memory of the people they represented. Something, anything, a smell, a touch, a word, but nothing came. They were cloudy, like smoke, and so he loved them in the way you love all beautiful things that flicker on the edge of what you can remember.

"My grandfather is my beginning, the only beginning I know," he whispered. "This should be my answer." But still, Gabriel did not know how to proceed. He started back toward the library.

As he walked down the path, he tried to think of his earliest memory. At first his grandfather's pipe tobacco filled his nostrils and the sound of a rocking chair creaking echoed in Gabriel's ears. A small breeze blew up and brought the bright smell of flowers to his nose. Suddenly there was another memory—one older than the others. "That's it!" he cried nearly shouting, and ran toward the library and into the garden, as the villagers all turned to gawk and murmur at the crazy stranger.

Passing the townspeople who had gathered to gossip about his absence and ignoring the Librarian who had already opened his mouth to criticize, he stopped abruptly in front of the stone. He grabbed a chisel and hammer from his satchel, shut his eyes and pounded into the stone.

The memory was vivid in his mind. Warm arms and soft hands, a smell like springtime and orange blossoms and finally a voice singing words he had no meaning for. The sound was like water falling. He felt warm and safe and loved. He banged the hammer into the pick and a chunk of stone fell away.

In his memory, his hands reached out to touch the person's face. He felt soft cheeks, a small earlobe, and a graceful neck. Gabriel continued chipping, while pieces of stone fell away.

The townspeople gawked and squealed, not bothering to lower their voices as they chattered. Gabriel continued working through the afternoon, pausing only to stare at the Librarian and say, "Ladder." The Librarian brought one and a tray of food. Gabriel took a quick drink of water, set the ladder up, shut his eyes, and once again began to work. He labored over the stone, his muscles straining while sweat ran down his back and soaked his shirt.

Long after the sun had set and the spectators had departed for their homes, Gabriel still kept working. He worked for three straight days, stopping only for water and ignoring the crowd that would grow in the morning and shrink at night. On the last day, an hour before sunrise, he was finished.

"It's perfect," a familiar voice called out. Gabriel turned to see the Gypsy standing and gazing upon the statue of a beautiful woman with a small boy on her lap. The woman's arms enfolded the child and they held a book in their hands. The boy looked excitedly at the pages, while the woman gazed lovingly at him. The Gypsy walked closer to Gabriel, noting his exhaustion. "It's amazing, they look so real."

"It's my mother—and me."

"I know."

"I didn't know her face until I started carving. I didn't remember what she looked like."

"Your hands remembered."

"Yes, that's why I had to shut my eyes to find her."

The Gypsy walked over to him, and placed her hand on his shoulder. "She's beautiful and it's clear she loved you so much. I'm sure she's proud, but you my friend, look ready to collapse. You need food, rest, and a bath. And tomorrow you come back and make that Librarian hand you every single gold piece he owes you in front of all those horrid villagers." Her eyes gleamed mischievously

Gabriel laughed, the sound was loud and bright. "That sounds great, you lead the way." The Gypsy gave a smile and linked her arm through his. So as the sky began to blossom from deep purple to pink, Gabriel and the Gypsy walked arm in arm, through the quiet streets and back to the inn.

Traveling many miles, Sebastian followed the river as it changed slowly from solid ice to rolling water. The river's rushing waters were like a song daring him to follow. Tree branches moved in the breeze and the forest's dark grayness turned a deep, leafy green. The smell of dirt and rain filled Sebastian's nostrils. An eerie mist clung to the trees, and haunting sounds, like ghostly whispers, echoed from all directions.

Up ahead the trees made a thick curtain. Pushing the leaves aside, he found himself in a swamp. Muddy ground surrounded a small lagoon, thick and green--like pea soup that's sat in a kettle for too long. Spreading from the lagoon were hundreds of long, wrapping vines.

With each step Sebastian took, the whispering grew louder. The vines began to move. They turned to reveal snake heads with long, slithering tongues. Slowly, they inched toward Sebastian with beady eyes fixed on their prey.

The whispering snakes struck and Sebastian cried out *"Mórathrú tobann!"* Instead of fangs piercing into Sebastian from all sides, tiny worms rained down. Many began to cling to his cloak. *"Lig dul,"* he said calmly and the squirming creatures fell to the ground. He crushed them beneath his boots as he strode to the edge of the murky lagoon. Bubbles formed in the water and something began to rise out of its center.

Music filled the air. It was not a human voice, nor any recognizable instrument. There's no precise description for the sound. The closest comparison is to sunlight sparkling in deep water, or a warm, crackling fire on a winter's night. Its notes called the listener to them, creating an irresistible urge to follow—to surrender. The music was a candle and its listeners only moths.

The source of the music emerged from the lagoon with a splash. She was beautiful in an unsettling way, with long seaweed hair that fell in waves down her delicate arms. She wore a green gown so dark it was almost black, and her skin held a moonlight blue cast. Her gray eyes stared at Sebastian. She continued her song. He moved closer.

"*Dearmad. Dearmad dhuine,*" she called in a lilting voice. "*Déan dearmad go léir.*"

"*Stad,*" he answered forcefully. She looked puzzled for a moment and stopped singing. "Swamp Witch, your spells have no effect on me."

An odd glimmer filled the Swamp Witch's eyes and a smile touched her lips. She looked him over carefully as though searching for something in particular.

"*T'is the rare traveler who comes along,
That can resist my siren's song,*" she murmured.

"I've come to seek your counsel," replied Sebastian.

"*If such a great wizard you be,
what is it you need from me?*"

"They say you know every spell that exists, in every language that has ever been--that you know of all the magical relics that have ever existed, and every potion it is possible to make."

"If knowledge is power then it is true,
I am far more powerful than you."

"I've been searching for the perfect spell—one that can bring something to life that has never been alive."

The Swamp Witch paused for a moment, considering his request.

"That is a task most unwise
for a mortal man to try.
The Gods alone have done this deed,
when they brought forth a single seed,
from which all life was forced to grow
and such it was and so it goes."

"But there must be a way!" cried out Sebastian.
The Swamp Witch tilted her head, giving him a piercing look.

"T'is true all things can be,
such are the rules of destiny.
But what is in this quest for me,
if I should solve your mystery?"

"Name your price. Anything it is in my power to do, I will," Sebastian answered firmly.

She ran her long nails over her chin and replied,

"Both beauty and terror go in its wake
and that is what I wish to take.
I will tell you what you need
to complete your irksome deed,
if you will in my hand set,
your most treasured amulet."

Sebastian's hand immediately jumped to his chest. Well hidden beneath his cloak and shirt, on a long leather chord, was the medallion he had stolen on that night in the fishing village. He was suddenly aware of its heavy weight against his skin. Panic raced through Sebastian. Could he possibly part with his most cherished possession? What would he do without it? What about the ice maiden? Was she worth the sacrifice? *I must have her*, he thought. *She must be mine.*

The Swamp Witch moved closer to Sebastian and opened her palm. Taking a deep breath, he lifted his hands to the cord. The medallion seemed to grow heavier and warmer, as though it couldn't bear to be parted from him. Quickly, he removed it, and placed it in the Swamp Witch's waiting hand.

Her mouth opened into a grin like the crescent moon, as she clutched the medallion tightly.

"For what you wish there is but one,
who can bring life where there was none.
He who takes can also give
and thus bestow a will to live.
Go to the edge of the forest trees,
where the dark lake meets the sea.
Down a path of broken stones,
past a well that's filled with bones,
hidden by thorny trees,
there a ruined castle be.
Across its moat and in its tower,
you'll find the one who has the power."

The Swamp Witch moved back toward the center of the lagoon.

"Who is he? What kind of magic does he possess? Why do I not know of him?" demanded Sebastian.

"His name is lost to human ears,
and so it's been for many years.
His magic is beyond the scope,
Of any foolish mortal's hopes."

She slipped quickly below the surface of the water. Waves rippled out, touching the edges of the lagoon, and then the water was still.

Alone, Sebastian felt a strange sensation. A sense of hollowness filled him and yet, at the same time, it was as though a heavy burden had been lifted. It was an odd mix of regret and relief. He brushed away his feelings about losing his medallion and focused instead on his goal. *I will find that castle and the one who can help me. Then she will be mine.* Sebastian began walking toward the edge of the forest and the adventure that awaited him.

Gabriel was awakened by a loud knocking on his door.

"Rise and shine," called the Gypsy.

"Wha—What," answered Gabriel sleepily. Running his fingers through his hair, he climbed out of bed, stumbled to the door, and opened it.

"I've come to warn you."

"What?" he repeated drowsily.

"You have about ten minutes before a huge group of villagers start pounding on your door."

"They hated my statue that much?" he asked horrified.

The Gypsy shook her head and laughed at him. "No idiot, they loved it—particularly the Mayor's wife. As disappointing as it is, you won't be getting your well-deserved gold from the Librarian. Instead, the Mayor wants to present it to you. He has some elaborate ceremony and unveiling planned. Villagers do love those kinds of things--any excuse for a celebration—I swear every time they paint a new sign, people are breaking out the ale." The Gypsy gave him a knowing wink. "If you get ready fast enough you can make it out of here before they show up. I'll see you there."

The Gypsy left and shut the door with a bang, bringing Gabriel out of his stupor. "A ceremony?" Gabriel asked the empty room. "For me?"

Gabriel got ready as quickly as possible and headed to the library. When he arrived, he found it decorated with colorful ribbons of yellow, orange and red. The library was teeming with villagers, who followed Gabriel, as he walked out to the garden and to his statue, which was now covered with a sparkling golden cloth.

"Here he is, the man of the hour!" called out a boisterous voice. Gabriel turned to face a short man with a large round belly and skin the color of cherry tree bark. The man walked over to Gabriel, shook his hand, and gave him a strong pat on the back. "Nice to meet you m'boy. I'm the Mayor of this wonderful little village. I got a sneak peek at your statue here. Wonderful job, my man, just wonderful! And now that you're here we can commence with the ceremony."

The Mayor and his wife stood in front of the covered statue. "My fellow villagers, this is a momentous occasion—a wonderful, stupendous occasion. At long last we have a statue for our Library!" The Mayor droned on for a bit longer about the wonderfulness of the statue and then called Gabriel forward.

"This great man has created a true work of art for us, one that we can enjoy for years to come." With a flourish the Mayor pulled off the gold cloth to reveal the statue. There was ooing and ahhing followed by applause and whistles. The Mayor motioned with his hands to quiet the crowd.

"In appreciation for your wonderful work, we give you sixty gold coins and this engraved pocket watch."

Gabriel accepted the gifts, nodded his head, and replied "Thank you," then tucked them into his pocket.

"Wonderful," answered the Mayor. "Now let's eat!" The villagers cheered and the feasting began. The smell of roasted meat and sweet pastries perfumed the air. Music played and Gabriel followed the lively sounds.

In a far corner of the garden, just beyond the circle of benches, were three musicians. One was playing a flute, another, a guitar, and the third, a fiddle. Gabriel watched as the fiddle player slid his fingers skillfully over the strings. A pang of sorrow moved through him as the ice maiden's face flashed in his mind.

Then a voice joined the song and Gabriel turned to see the Gypsy singing.

> *"Long ago on a summer's day,*
> *I stole a ship and sailed away.*
> *Across the sea for many moons,*
> *To find my way at last to you.*
> *Heigh-lo, heigh-lo and tally-oh,*
> *alas it's time for me to go,*
> *one day I shall return to you,*
> *heigh-lo, heigh-lo and tally-oo."*

The song finished and the listeners applauded. The players began another tune.

"That was lovely. You have a beautiful voice," Gabriel said to the Gypsy.

"Thank you. It's an old song." The Gypsy looked at him thoughtfully. "I noticed you were watching the fiddler very closely. You miss playing, don't you?"

"Yes—no, I mean I *used* to play. I told you I gave it up."

"Seems silly to give up something that means a lot to you," the Gypsy argued.

"I, well it's hard to explain. But it's beside the point since I left my fiddle behind."

"Well that's easy enough to fix." She flashed him a smile and ran over to the fiddler. She whispered something in his ear and he nodded his head. He handed her his fiddle and hushed his fellow musicians. The Gypsy returned to Gabriel, and gave him the instrument. "Your turn."

"I can't play those songs."

"I've heard all those songs before. I'd much rather hear yours."

Gabriel took a deep breath and raised the fiddle to his chin. He shut his eyes, paused for a moment, and then began to play. The song was slow and winding, a sad melody, like wind blowing on a frozen lake, or whispers in a dream. Around him a crowd of villagers stopped to listen. The song was full of longing and sadness, like a wish waiting to be granted.

Gabriel saw in his mind the frozen stare of the ice maiden. When he opened his eyes, he met the Gypsy's gaze. She looked so warm in the afternoon light, and her beautiful eyes sparkled with unshed tears. His song changed. The melody became more welcoming— comforting, like a warm breeze, or a sunset. The Gypsy and Gabriel watched each other intently.

The song finished with a loud crescendo and the spectators responded with enthusiastic applause. The musicians let out a cheer, then the flute and guitar players began a folk tune and the villagers danced.

The Gypsy held out her hand to Gabriel and he took it in his own. He felt her skin warm beneath his fingers. Hand in hand they walked to a stone bench in the corner of the garden. They sat quietly together while all around them the villagers danced and the afternoon light dimmed to amber.

4

DREAMS & WISHES

After several days of hiking through the woods, Sebastian arrived at the dark lake. By now the sun had set and the moon hung low in the sky, its light streaming through wispy, gray clouds. There was no wind, no sound of bird or beast. The water on the lake was still.

The world was so calm and quiet, Sebastian decided to rest. Wearily, he sat down on the rocky soil several feet from the water's edge, and leaned against a tree. Closing his eyes, he fell into a troubled slumber.

Sebastian dreamt he was back at the docks of the fishing village. This time, there was one gigantic wave that grew larger and larger until it covered the entire sky. It crashed down over him. Sebastian opened his mouth to scream, but instead of sound spilling out, water filled his throat.

Awaking, Sebastian felt his surroundings were different. The air was thicker than air should be and the world was heavy. A rushing sound filled his ears. When he opened his eyes they met the sting of water. There was no air, he could not breathe. His lungs burned and the sound of his own heartbeat echoed in his ears. *I'm dying*, thought Sebastian; *I'm drowning in the lake.*

Thrashing his arms, he struggled to escape. Tightness gripped his chest. The sound of his heart grew faster and louder, like the ticking of clock that's wound too tightly. Struggling and fighting, Sebastian propelled himself upward. He needed air---needed to breathe—*Up, Up, Up*—his mind pounding out the words in a frantic chorus. In what seemed like hours, but was only seconds, Sebastian pierced through the water's surface, gasping for air.

Before he could feel relief at having escaped a watery death, he was dragged under again. Long tentacles circled his limbs. Slimy and thick, they tightened and pulled until he felt like he was being splintered into a million pieces. Sebastian struggled futilely as the creature in the lake pulled him even lower.

I must get out, I must get out! Out! he thought. *Saor mé,* he repeated over and over in his mind. The creature released his hold and Sebastian burst from the lake. The sound of his heart thumping echoed in his ears, as his arms thrashed through the dark water and toward the shore. Coughing and still wet, he pulled himself to the rocky ground where he'd fallen asleep. *That thing must have dragged me into the lake while I was sleeping...I have to get away.*

Shivering and disoriented, he stumbled through the woods trying to put as much distance as possible between himself and the lake. After some time, he found a huge, gnarled tree that looked as though it would hide him well enough and collapsed behind it.

Sebastian awoke to see sunlight falling through the trees and wondered momentarily if he'd dreamt the entire ordeal, but the tear in his pants and his missing satchel confirmed the truth. Gone were his food rations and everything he'd brought with him for the journey, except the chisel he'd stolen from the mountain cabin. Tucked safely in his cloak pocket, it had somehow survived his struggle in the lake.

His stomach grumbling with hunger, Sebastian spent the morning searching for food. He knew if he used his magic so soon after his spell in the lake, he'd be left weak and defenseless for whatever obstacle lay ahead of him. He tried to hunt, but found no animals anywhere in the forest. He searched for some kind of edible fruit or vegetable, and after several hours found three bushes filled with small orange nuts. He ate several handfuls and filled his pockets with the rest. Rummaging through the leaves, he noticed something silver lying in the dirt behind the bush. He moved closer and bent low to the ground.

It was a jagged rock, too large and heavy to be moved. Gleaming brightly in the sunlight it was engraved with the letter "*C*." Looking around he saw another stone a few feet away. This one also possessed a curious letter engraving. This time the letter was "*U.*" *This must be the path of broken stones the Swamp Witch had mentioned*, he thought. *What do the letters mean? Is it some kind of spell?*

Sebastian continued along the path and each stone he found revealed another letter. He followed them all, noting each letter until there were no more stones. He spoke aloud the curious word they spelled, "*Cuimhnigh*," said Sebastian. "Remember?" he translated, "Remember what? What is there worth remembering?"

The ice maiden's image appeared in his mind and he felt a rush of longing. *No matter how unreachable she seems--I'll make her real*, he thought. *She's not stronger than me—no one is stronger than me.*

A memory flashed in Sebastian's mind.

"We'll get ya!" called the tall boy. He was running alongside two other boys, one had curly yellow hair and the other wore bright red mittens. "Ya won't get away from us!"

Sebastian was about eight years old and running through the snow. Since he was younger and smaller than the other three boys they caught up to him quickly—no matter how fast he ran, they always managed to catch him and today was no different. The tall boy grabbed the end of Sebastian's scarf and immediately he fell back, the scarf choking him. Coughing, he lay on the ground, struggling to breathe.

"What the matter? Cat got ya tongue?" the curly haired boy asked as they peered down at him.

"Poor li'l baby, why don't ya go cry to ya momma?" said the boy with the red mittens. "Oh that's right, ya don't have a momma!"

"I bet his momma couldn't stand him either!" laughed the tall boy, as he tugged harder on the scarf. "What do ya fellas think we should do to him?"

The young Sebastian's gaze grew hard. Anger burned inside him and formed a hot, angry knot in his stomach. Why did they torture him? He was smaller than they were—and there were three of them and one of him. Why did they get such enjoyment out of hurting him? He'd learned not to cry. After the time they'd hit him right on the jaw with a well thrown stone and laughed at the blood that dripped from his face, he vowed he'd never give them the satisfaction of tears. And if he went home crying and hurt, his grandmother would whip him for being a "cry baby" and he'd have to face another of her "punishments." Tears were simply a luxury the young Sebastian could not afford.

If I was bigger and stronger, I'd show them, he thought. He wished with all his strength for them to hurt and to suffer and for him to be the cause of their misery. *I wish they would know what it's like to be chased and hurt and scared...*

As if answering the young boy's wish, a loud noise filled the air, like the sound of heavy winds blowing against boat sails. Black objects began to fill the sky, coming closer to the boys. The sound grew louder and the wind stronger. Crows swooped down, attacking the three tormentors. The boys screamed and ran as the birds pecked at their heads, necks, and arms. Hundreds of crows swarmed and chased the boys, while Sebastian watched in horrified disbelief. All the crows but one followed the boys as they ran into the distance.

The one remaining crow landed in the snow in front of Sebastian. The bird moved closer and stood unusually still. He stared directly into the boy's eyes, bowed his head, and flew off.

Dazed, Sebastian unwound the scarf from around his neck. He tried to understand what he'd just seen—what had just happened. Was it possible his wish had summoned the crows? If he wasn't the cause, why hadn't the crows attacked him? Why had that one crow stayed behind?

He must have called to the birds with his wish. Sebastian imagined for a moment how hurt and frightened the boys' must be, and felt pity surge inside him. He pictured the crows pecking into the boys' skin and drawing blood. His stomach churned as he realized what he'd done.

Just then, he glanced down at the scarf in his hands, and remembered how the boys had dragged him to the ground, remembered the way the scarf felt as it dug into his skin, remembered how afraid he'd been on the ground, unable breathe, as their smirking faces stared down at him. He knew all they were thinking about was how they'd torture him next.

The boys' words screamed in his ears "*I bet his momma couldn't stand him either.*" The pity was gone. All Sebastian felt was that hard knot in his stomach.

And this time when he imagined the boys being tortured, a smile crossed his face.

Nonsense, thought Sebastian, breaking out of the memory. *These stones must have a worthless memory charm attached to them. Enough foolishness. There's too much to do.*

Sebastian continued past the stones and climbed down a small ravine. There were no plants there at all and the few trees were black and dead. The earth was dry and scorched as if it were a desert instead of an open clearing at the edge of a forest. There was still no sign of any animals, not even the far away cry of woodland bird—just a barren space. *There must have been a fire here recently,* he thought.

Sebastian walked forward and noticed more stones a few yards behind a blackened tree stump. Moving closer to examine it, he noticed that round grey stones were set in a circle. It was a well. The Swamp Witch's words echoed back to him, *"Down a path of broken stones, past a well that's filled with bones."* Sebastian peered inside the structure and sure enough it was piled high with bones.

The black gaping eyes of human and animal skulls stared back at Sebastian. He smelled something odd, similar to the odor a match makes the second it strikes a hard surface. Fear shot through him like lightning. His entire body tensed. With no time to think, he jumped into the well, landing on the bones with a loud crunch. Above him, a blanket of fire appeared. Sweat streamed down his face as the flames grew closer.

"Thoghairm oighear!" he screamed and a thick impenetrable layer of ice covered the top of the well. His body shook and his breath came in quick gulps. Sebastian suddenly knew what made the forest uninhabitable. Feverishly he thought of all the spells and charms he'd ever known.

The layer of ice had given Sebastian a few precious moments. That was all the time he'd get to figure out how to slay a Dragon.

"Finally!" Casper called out. "Now this story is going somewhere!" Before Johanna could respond to her brother, a ringing filled the room.

"Ah, that's the phone, children. Most likely your mother calling to check on you," said Mrs. Kinder, as she rose from her seat and went down the small hallway into her kitchen.

Johanna thought it odd that she took the book with her. *Is there a reason she doesn't want me to see it?* Johanna wondered. She moved toward the doorway, with Casper close behind. They listened intently to the conversation.

"Hello, Emily. We're having a lovely time. No worries my dear, they are on their best behavior." Mrs. Kinder let out a laugh. "Yes, even Casper."

Johanna shot Casper a quick look and he simply shrugged his shoulders in response.

"How is he doing?" Mrs. Kinder asked, then paused to listen to the answer from Johanna and Casper's mother. "Well, you know how doctors are, always making everything so complicated. I'm sure it will all be just fine. And don't worry one bit about the children. We're having a lovely time." She paused again. "No need to mention it at all. You're doing me a favor as well—it's nice for an old woman like me to have some company. They can help me with dinner."

"Did you hear that?" Casper exclaimed. "Dinner! She's going to turn us into dinner."

"Shut up Casper! I need to hear this!" Johanna answered, but by then Mrs. Kinder had already hung up the phone and was returning to the sitting room.

"Well children, we're going to get started on dinner. Your mother is going to be a little later than expected."

"Why?" Johanna asked. "What's wrong?"

Mrs. Kinder eyes held an odd glint when she answered. "Nothing to worry about. Things are just taking a while at the hospital, but she'll be on her way as soon as she can." Mrs. Kinder's tone lightened and she continued, "So have either of you had goulash before?

"Ghoul-ash?" Casper questioned. "Seriously?"

Mrs. Kinder's mouth turned up into a slight smile. "I assure you Casper no ghouls are used in my recipe. Now follow me and we'll get started."

"What about the story?" asked Johanna.

"Lucky for you that I can read a story and cook at the same time." Mrs. Kinder winked and turned back toward the kitchen.

Johanna and Casper followed through the small hallway. The kitchen seemed a bit brighter than the rest of the house. The walls were covered in white rectangular tiles, some chipped from the passage of time. There was a round wooden table surrounded by four chairs and covered with a lace tablecloth. The cupboards were white and had paint missing in some spots. They had a cut out trim—the kind that reminded Johanna of gingerbread houses. There were odd little knickknacks interspersed throughout, like owl salt and pepper shakers whose round saucer eyes were in a constant state of surprise, or a clock in the shape of a cat who's tail and eyeballs moved eerily back and forth, but the thing that stood out most to the children was the large, black stove. Standing there ominously, it seemed as though it had jumped right out from the Witch's house in Hansel and Gretel.

Casper stood staring, his mouth agape. Johanna elbowed him and still he let out no response.

"Ah you've seen my stove. Isn't it lovely—it's an antique."

"Yes," Casper said, his voice trailing. "Lovely." He turned his head to gaze intently at his sister, giving her a clear you're-the-older-sister-and-you're supposed-to-save-me-look.

Mrs. Kinder turned away from them and grabbed the gingham apron that was hanging near the hook by the stove and put it on.

"We have to get out of here," Casper whispered to Johanna.

"Just calm down already," Johanna whispered back.

When Mrs. Kinder turned back she was holding a large knife in one hand.

"Nooo!" screamed Casper, falling back and landing on his backside.

"Oh, don't worry dear, I wasn't going to let you use the knife," Mrs. Kinder said. "You can use the peeler." She turned around and opened a drawer.

"Get up," Johanna whispered, pulling Casper to his feet.

"Here," Mrs. Kinder said, placing a peeler and a small bowl of potatoes on the table. "You sit here Casper and you can put the leftover peels in the bowl. Johanna, I think you can handle a smaller knife." She placed a small paring knife, a small black bowl, and a cutting board on the table next to another chair. "Johanna, you sit over here and take care of cutting the carrots—do be careful dear, you don't want to chop off one of your fingers instead."

"What about you?" asked Casper, his eyes narrowing.

"I'm handling the meat." Mrs. Kinder answered triumphantly pulling a very bloody looking piece of meat out of the sink and slapping it on to the cutting board next to the counter. The children jumped a bit in response. Mrs. Kinder wiped her hands on her apron and grabbed the golden book from the counter next to the sink. She placed it an iron cookbook stand, angled toward her, but away from the children.

How can she read the book and chop the meat at the same time? Johanna wondered. Mrs. Kinder took a quick glance at the book, and then began hacking into the meat.

"Since we're all busy working, I think now's the perfect time to get back to our story. Let's see...I think its Gabriel's turn now."

Back at the lemon village, night was coming to a close and morning prepared to blanket the sky. At this late hour, Gabriel walked the Gypsy to her room and stood outside her door.

"What will you do now that you've finished the statue?" asked the Gypsy.

"I'm not sure," he answered. "But I know that I don't wish to leave you."

The Gypsy shook her head. "Wishes are powerful things—take care when you make them. You don't know what it might mean should that wish come true."

"Do you want me to leave?" he asked carefully.

"My wants cannot change what is."

"But my choices can and I choose to be with you," he argued.

She gave him one of the smiles that had become so achingly familiar now, but sadness glinted in her eyes. "Some choices aren't ours to make. You were on a journey before we met. The world won't let you abandon it easily."

"The world doesn't matter to me—I won't leave you, unless you tell me to go," answered Gabriel passionately. "And if you leave I'll follow you. If that isn't what you want, tell me so."

She took his hand in her own. "You don't understand. If it was just a matter of what I wanted—I can't" she stopped abruptly and touched his face. "Your heart will lead you where you're meant to go. If nothing else, trust in that."

"Then if I must go, come with me."

"I can't. No matter how much I might want to— "

"Yes, you can—" Gabriel argued.

"You have to trust me, Gabriel."

"Don't I always? Why can't you trust me— "

"Please, Gabriel. We're both tired and we should rest." The Gypsy answered, her voice sounding sad and distant. "We'll talk more about this later. But for now, let's just say goodnight."

As she turned to go, Gabriel asked, "You won't disappear now, will you? You'll still be here tomorrow?"

"I'll be here." The Gypsy nodded then turned away, stepping into her room and shutting the door behind her.

Gabriel climbed the spiral staircase to his room. The warmth and happiness he'd felt from the celebration dimmed. Why did the Gypsy seem so sad? Why did she insist that he wasn't meant to stay? If he must leave, why couldn't she come with him? So many questions ran through his mind as he fell into an uneasy sleep.

Gabriel was back in the village by the Frozen Forest. There were no people--all the homes and shops were encased in layers of ice. He shivered as cold winds blew around him. Someone or something was crying deep, painful sobs that echoed from all directions. Desperately, Gabriel searched for the source of the sound. A voice called out from behind him, "Help me." He turned and faced the ice maiden. "Help me," she said in a voice that sounded like wind, "Please." As Gabriel reached for her, he awoke.

Gabriel knew then that the Gypsy was right and his journey wasn't over. He couldn't stay in the lemon village any longer, but there was something he needed to do before he could leave. He rushed into town to finish the task.

That evening Gabriel went to the Gypsy's room, but there was no answer to his knock, so he sat in the tavern and waited for her. Each hour that passed with no sign of her, his worry grew. Finally, when the tavern was empty and he was ready to leave, the Gypsy entered and sat across from him.

"I've been waiting for you," he said.

"I know, I'm sorry. There were some things I needed to take care of," she answered.

"You were right, I can't stay here," he paused and continued, "The ice maiden I told you about—she needs me."

"I know that too," she replied.

"She's begging me to rescue her, only I don't know how."

"If you had all the power in the world, what would you do for her?" asked the Gypsy.

"I'd give her life—make her real."

"Well then, that's what you have to do."

"How can I? Is that even possible?" he asked.

"Never doubt for even a moment that anything is possible," answered the Gypsy.

"I can't bring something to life."

"Seems to me you've come pretty close to that already—you just need some help to finish what you started."

"But I'm no magician or philosopher—I can't turn ice to flesh and blood."

"Then you need to find something or someone who can."

"Is that even possible? Where would I even start looking for someone who can do such a thing?" Gabriel shook his head and gave her a small smile. "I seem to always be asking you where I should begin, and somehow you always know the answer."

She tilted her head and returned his grin. "And I do this time as well. I've heard stories about a relic, one powerful enough to make miracles, but cursed enough that catastrophe follows wherever it goes. They say that wherever there's been a disaster, it's been there first. I can't tell you where to find it or even what it is, but I do know of someone who might be able to. Deep in the Frozen Forest—in the coldest most barren corner of it, lives a goblin. He's the guardian of lost and forgotten things, and he may be able to help you find it."

"I know that forest well, why have I never seen him?"

"You must go to him and call out some magic words. He's a trickster and will try to frighten you— but it's all a game to him. He won't hurt you, but he won't help you for free either." She pulled a peacock feather from her hair and gave it to Gabriel. "Give him this and tell him that I sent you. He owes me a favor."

"Where in the forest do I find him?" asked Gabriel.

"Far into the woods—near the forest edge, there's a large pile of rocks with many small openings. Stand in front of it and yell the words *thoghairm coimeádaí.*"

"*Thooog..hair..mah comeda,*" he repeated.

"*Thoghairm coimeádaí,*" the Gypsy answered slowly.

"*Thoghairm--*" Gabriel responded, carefully repeating her words. "*Coimeádaí*"

"That's exactly right. Say it just that way. And remember he'll try to scare you, but it's all for show. Just show him the feather and tell him I sent you."

"That's all I have to do?" he asked.

"Well that's all there is to meeting the goblin, but that's only the beginning of your quest."

"What else should I know? I've never met a goblin or anything magical—except for you."

"I'm not magical—just a fortune-teller, no more, no less. Which reminds me, we have some unfinished business to take care of—I'll need your hand," she said firmly. Gabriel did as she asked. The Gypsy turned his palm face up and studied it for several minutes, running her fingers carefully over the lines, scars, and calluses.

"Your journey will be long and hard, so you must remember to be brave. Your allies and enemies will not always be as clear as you presume. Your past is linked to your future—they are a broken circle that seeks completion."

She looked up from his palm and continued. "The way you came is not the way you should return." She continued, "There is a fishing boat waiting for you at the docks just outside of town. It has bright blue sails painted with a large sun. It will take you to a small fishing village. From there it's a short journey to the Frozen Forest."

Gabriel turned his palm over and squeezed the Gypsy's hand. "I've no way to thank you for everything you've done for me."

"There is no need, Gabriel."

"Still, I wanted to do something for you—it's small really." Gabriel reached into his satchel and pulled out a beautifully carved rose. It was made of a dark cherry wood and was so lifelike you could almost smell the rose's perfume.

The Gypsy took it in her hands and tears shimmered in her eyes. "No one's ever given me anything like this. Thank you."

"Now you'll have something to remember me by."

She smiled. "As though I could forget."

"Come with me." Gabriel urged. "I know it's dangerous, but I'll keep you safe, I promise—"

"It's not that, Gabriel. I can't leave. This is your journey and you must finish it." The Gypsy wiped the tears from the corner of her eyes and composed herself. "Now enough of this, destiny is waiting for you and I've held you up far too long."

Gabriel brought the Gypsy's hand to his lips and gave it a soft kiss. He stood and looked into her eyes. "I may not be able to read palms or tell fortunes, but I know, without even the tiniest bit of uncertainty, that this is not goodbye. We will meet again."

"Til then," the Gypsy whispered and gave Gabriel a soft smile. Then, he was gone.

"No!" cried Johanna. "It can't be!" She threw a carrot into the bowl in disgust.

"What's the matter?" asked Mrs. Kinder.

"He can't leave the Gypsy!" exclaimed Johanna.

"Of course, Johanna has to be upset about the lovey-dovey girl stuff," replied Casper, rolling his eyes.

Johanna ignored Casper. "It isn't right. They're supposed to be together!"

"Who said they were supposed to be together?" replied Mrs. Kinder, as she dumped chunks of meat into a large stewpot, using a wooden spoon to move them around.

"They just are. It can't be goodbye." Johanna said firmly.

"Goodbyes are important you know. Nothing new can start unless something ends," Mrs. Kinder answered.

"I guess if you look at it that way..." Johanna responded, unconvinced.

"Enough sad stuff! It's Sorcerer time! You said dragon—you *promised* me a dragon and I finished peeling *all* those potatoes already."

"There were like five," Johanna answered.

"Five is a lot to peel." Johanna rolled her eyes and Casper continued. "I have smaller fingers than you. Anyway, I've earned a break from all the love junk—I want some action."

"Of course all you care about is fighting and dragons," said Johanna.

"No, you're *wrong*. I care about magic too—and PIRATES," said Casper with extra emphasis.

"Well then," said Mrs. Kinder cheerfully as he dumped a can of tomatoes into her stew pot. "I believe we left Sebastian in quite a pickle—what was it again, ah yes, he was getting ready to fight a dragon."

Sebastian's breath burned in his throat and his mouth felt unbearably dry. *Is this it,* he wondered, *is this how it ends? Is this how I end?* Through the thick ice, an enormous head peered down. Despite the ice and bright flames many feet above him, Sebastian could clearly see the dragon's steadfast yellow eyes staring down at him.

Drops splattered onto Sebastian's head as the ice began to melt under the dragon's fiery breath. Searching his mind for a way to escape, Sebastian stared at the gruesome face peering down at him through the ice. *Ice—yes ice!*

"*Thoghairm stoirm oighear*", he shouted. The sound--loud and desperate, as it echoed against the stones. "*Thoghairm stoirm oighear!*" Thunderous crashing echoed above Sebastian and the ground shook. He felt as though he were inside of a large drum being pounded from all sides. The rumbling continued for several minutes, making the bones beneath him rattle and dance. Then everything stopped. All was quiet.

The narrow well grew suddenly chilly. Sebastian shivered, his breath making little white clouds in the air. He tensed for a few moments, waiting for some kind of noise—some sign of danger—any small detail that would tell him whether he was safe or damned, but none came. The world remained still.

As he struggled to stand, Sebastian's legs sank unsteadily into the pile of bones beneath him. His voice trembled as he said, "*Staighre thoghairm.*" With a creaking sound, the stones in front of him pushed out and turned into a staircase. Carefully he climbed, until he reached the ice ceiling. Placing his palm against the surface above him, he felt the ice burning against his flesh.

Sebastian took a deep breath and spoke one word, "*Leá.*" The ice melted and water rushed over him. He reached up, his fingers grasping the side of the well. Trying not to slip on the damp rock, he struggled to pull himself up and over the edge. After a few moments, he climbed over the side and stood upright. He shivered as the chilly air pressed against his wet clothes.

All around, the ground, the tree stumps, the dead branches, everything, was covered in ice. Standing directly in front of Sebastian was a sight very few in any world have ever seen before: a completely frozen dragon. There was a gruesome beauty to the creature now—as though someone had taken the fire-breathing monster and dipped him into crystal. The dragon's dark red and purple scales sparkled in the sunlight, his giant wings were opened as if he were preparing to take flight and his long, spiked tail was curled in the air, stopped in mid-swing. Most terrifying was the dragon's large gaping jaws, filled with black fangs the size of fire logs, frozen as if it were ready to unleash a huge fireball. The dragon was as still as everything else around him. His eyes stared unblinking at Sebastian.

A sense of relief filled Sebastian—his spell had worked! He had summoned an ice storm, and it had been strong enough to freeze the dragon. *I should never have doubted myself,* he thought.

"Now it's time to finish this." Sebastian whispered to himself.

Reaching into his pocket, Sebastian pulled out the remainder of the orange nuts left over from the morning. Tossing a few on the ground, he said in a voice as cold as the ice that covered the dragon, "*Mórathrú tobann bollán*". Instantly, the small nuts grew into large boulders. Sebastian stepped back from the dragon to stand behind the well. Staring the Dragon grimly in the eyes, he felt a momentary twinge in his heart—like when you unexpectedly prick your finger on a thorn or needle. The dragon was ferocious, but noble. Though Sebastian wouldn't admit it, deep inside him there was regret at having to destroy something so grand. But as suddenly as that little spark glimmered, was as quickly as Sebastian extinguished it. With the last of his strength, he shouted, "*Briseadh!*"

The large boulders flew through the air striking the dragon from all sides. Like a mirror falling to the ground, the dragon shattered into millions of icy shards. All that remained of the once great dragon were scattered bits of red and purple.

Feeling dizzy, Sebastian fell to his knees. Exhaustion was taking over, leaving him no choice but to succumb. He cursed the fact that his power demanded so much from him. *I single-handedly bested a Dragon— what could I do if my powers didn't leave me so weak?* Sebastian had just one more thought before unconsciousness swallowed him. *What was so strong it could use something as powerful as a Dragon for protection?*

5

DEATH & LOSS

At the docks of the lemon village, Gabriel saw the ship. It was constructed from a strange green wood that looked more like moss than solid lumber. The vessel was much larger than any other boats moored in the harbor. Its sails were bright blue and the topsail was painted with a gleaming orange sun that sparkled in the early morning light.

Gabriel walked down the creaking dock and toward the ship. Moving closer to the bow, he paused to examine the ship's figurehead. It was an intricate carving of a mermaid with long, flowing hair and a teasing smile. Her eyes gazed at the sky as though searching for something. Somehow, she seemed familiar to him. As he stared, the figurehead's face changed to reveal a smile he knew so well. "Gypsy! It can't be you!" he exclaimed.

"Heigh-ho! Who goes there?" called out a deep voice, breaking Gabriel's reverie. He looked up and now standing at the bow of the ship was a young man with olive-colored skin, a dark stubbly beard and long hair tied behind his head with a leather cord. Gabriel glanced back at the figurehead, but she wasn't smiling and no longer resembled the Gypsy. He ignored the small ache in his heart and turned his attention to the sailor.

"Good day! I'm Gabriel," he answered. The sailor stood with his arms across his chest. His white shirt-sleeves were rolled up, revealing his tanned and muscular arms. On his left forearm was a sun tattoo that matched the marking on the sail.

"So, you're the one I've been waitin' on. Come aboard, the wind's gettin' restless and so am I," called the sailor.

"How did you know I was coming?" Gabriel asked as he climbed up the gangplank.

"The Gypsy asked me to take you to the fishin' village across the sea." Gabriel felt that same hint of sadness pulse inside him at the mention of the Gypsy. *So, that's why she kept me waiting,* he thought, *she was meeting with him.*

"How do you know the Gypsy?" Gabriel asked, his voice taking on a tinge of hostility.

The sailor eyed Gabriel with amusement in his eyes. "I could ask the same of you," he answered. Gabriel's eyes darkened and for a moment jealousy flared inside him. "I take it she didn't tell you who I am."

"No, she didn't. *I take it* you know each other very well," Gabriel answered with even more of an edge to his voice.

The sailor let out a deep, rumbling laugh, the sound as warm and fluid as melted gold. "I know her well enough to say she'd find this bit of jealousy from you quite amusin'."

"Jealousy—that's ridiculous—we're friends— "

The sailor cut him off and smiled, "Before you work yourself up any more than you already have, I'll end your worries. I'm her brother, Brishen, and she called in a hell of a lot of favors from me on your behalf. So, I'm thinkin' that she fancies you, or at the very least owes you quite a debt. So, which one is it?"

"I'm the one who's indebted to her."

"Then it seems she's taken a shine to you."

Gabriel felt a blush creeping into his cheeks as he fought off his embarrassment. "She's just kind—and we're friends."

Brishen rolled his eyes. "Yes, of course—so obvious, really. Don't know why I didn't catch that during all your huffin' and puffin'. Enough jabberin', like I said before the wind's restless, so it's best we're off--quick as silver. Now let me show you 'round my pride and joy, Grian's Kiss." Brishen banged his hands on the ship's side. "This here's the love of my life, nowhere in the world is there a more beautiful ship."

"I've never seen anything like it."

"I imagine not. She's made of magic wood—from a forest well on the other side of the world. A place very few people have ever laid eyes on." Brishen walked along the bow of the ship, motioning for Gabriel to follow.

"This is a magic ship?" Gabriel asked.

Brishen turned to face Gabriel. Brishen raised his eyebrows and looked intently at Gabriel. "You the type bothered by magic?"

"Not particularly, although it doesn't seem as though I have much of a choice in the matter these days. It's odd, for so long I never knew much about magic—I mean I knew that it existed—knew all the stories, but it wasn't part of my life. Now it's all around me."

"Magic can have a way of sneakin' up on you, when you least expect it. Love's like that too—or so I've heard." Brishen gave another laugh. "Been too busy explorin' to worry about women *too* much—although they've been a charmin' distraction from time to time—but I've sworn off love, at least 'til I'm too old to care about sailin'. I've seen many a cautious man trapped by love—it's the most dangerous kind of magic."

"Speaking of men, where's the crew? A ship this big should have at least a few crew members," asked Gabriel. In response, Brishen lifted his fingers to his mouth and let out a high piercing whistle.

A flapping sound filled the air and a large golden owl came down to rest on the Brishen's shoulder. "This here's my first mate, Owl. He's brave and fast and loyal—can't really ask for better company." Gabriel eyed the bird. With its golden feathers reflecting in the sunlight, the creature was magnificent. Owl stared at Gabriel as if trying to determine whether he was worthy to board the ship. Brishen spoke cheerfully to the Owl. "There now mate, this here's the traveler I've been tellin' you about. We need to brin' him across the sea in one piece--else my sister will have my neck." Brishen stroked Owl's feathers. "Don't worry, he seem's a nice enough sort."

"That's your entire crew?" questioned Gabriel.

"The beauty of a magic ship is I don't need a crew—although dependin' on the voyage I may take some men on here and there. All I need to do is shout out the orders and the ship obeys. The only thin' it can't do is steer—that's up to me. Besides sailin' wouldn't be much fun if all I did was stare at the ocean for hours."

Brishen shouted out orders starting with "Pull up the anchor!" and continuing with "Secure the riggings." Gabriel stared wide-eyed as the anchor pulled itself up and the lines tightened themselves. It was like a ghost ship—only instead of a ghostly crew there was only Brishen and the solemn-eyed Owl.

"Is there anything I can do to help?" asked Gabriel. Brishen took his place behind the helm and Owl flew up and took roost in the crow's nest. "Just keep your eyes open for any trouble."

"Is there anything in particular I should be looking for?"

"I think you're smart enough to know trouble when you see it," Brishen answered with a smile. "At least I hope you are. Now there are lots of advantages to bein' at sea and the first one is I can sing as much as I want-- as loud as I please." So, with that, Brishen began singing countless sea shanties in his cheerful and booming voice, while Gabriel whittled mindlessly on a piece of wood he'd found on deck. There was a quality to Brishen's voice that was so like the Gypsy's, it was no

wonder Gabriel's heart ached when the tune changed
to one he'd heard before.

> *"Long ago on a summer's day,*
> *I stole a ship and sailed away.*
> *Across the sea for many moons,*
> *To find my way at last to you.*
> *Heigh-lo, heigh-lo and tally-oh,*
> *alas it's time for me to go,*
> *one day I shall return to you,*
> *heigh-lo, heigh-lo and tally-oo."*

Gabriel remembered the Gypsy's sweet voice singing in the library's garden. Gabriel stared at the ocean
and spoke softly to himself, "Do you miss me? Is
Brishen right? Is it more than just friendship?" Gabriel
looked down in his hands and realized that he'd been
carving a peacock feather. He tucked it back into his
pocket.

"You're an odd one—mumblin' to yourself and def-
initely on the thoughtful side. I see why my sister has a
thin' for you. You probably don't mind it all when she
goes on and on with all her strange mumbo jumbo--"

"You know her name, don't you? She said there was
one person in the whole world who does. It must be
you," Gabriel blurted out.

"Aye, that's true. And don't go askin' me what it is—she'd kill me if I went around blabbin' it, even to you."

"All right, I'll try a different question. What was she like when you were young?"

"A colossal pain. You ever try to win a game of cards with a fortune teller?" Brishen let out a sigh. "For years, I couldn't hold onto a single coin, 'til finally I got wise enough and stopped playin' her for money."

"She's hiding something from me," Gabriel said suddenly. "Something besides just her name." Brishen glanced back at him.

"Aye, I'm guessin' she's hidden quite a bit from you. My sister's always been one to prefer talkin' about others than herself."

"Why is she so secretive?"

"Those are her secrets to tell—not mine. And I'm thinkin' if she wanted you to know she'd have told you herself. Then again, I also know that she must care for you since she went to the trouble of gettin' me to help you, so I'm guessin' she didn't want to burden you."

"Burden me? What burden could she possibly be? All she's ever done is help me. Is she in some kind of trouble?"

Brishen gave Gabriel a penetrating look. "As much as I would like to tell you—I can't."

"So, she has a big secret?" Gabriel asked, urgency lining his voice.

"She has lots of secrets—some bigger than others."

"You're avoiding the question."

"Yes." Brishen nodded in response. "Yes, I am."

"Please," Gabriel implored, "If she's in trouble I need to know— "

"She's not in danger if that's what you mean." Brishen let out a sigh. "I'm bound to this ship, the same way you're bound to your journey. She's bound as well—just in a bit of a different way than we are."

"Bound?"

"I mean she isn't free—she cannot follow her own wishes. The way that you can choose to see your quest through, the way that I can choose to man this ship— she has no choice."

"Explain!"

"I've said too much already—when the truth is ready to come out, it always finds a way. Now we've had far too much of this serious talk. Don't want you go burstin' into tears or anythin'." Brishen gave him a wink. "How about instead I tell you about the time I got stuck in a pub in just my skivvies with a dancin' monkey at my side?"

Without waiting for a response, Brishen continued with his story. "Well, it all started when I was on my way to a carnival out in the city beyond the mountains.

Along the way, I came to a farm where I met this farmer's daughter while she was putting up a scarecrow…" He continued the story 'til the sun went to sleep and the stars awoke.

Somewhere during the night and during Brishen's fourth or fifth story about dancing monkeys, Gabriel fell asleep propped up against a barrel on deck. He awoke to see the sun looming in the horizon. It cast pink, and tangerine colored light on the waves, making the water a moving kaleidoscope. Gabriel watched in awe as the colors became brighter and the sun rose.

"Beautiful, isn't it?" called Brishen. "There's nothin' like sunrise on the sea."

"Did you sleep at all?" asked Gabriel.

"I got a couple a winks while I was standin' at the helm. You sail long enough you learn to sleep standin' up."

Gabriel looked out and all he could see was a vast ocean. No signs of land or other ships. "How far are we from the village?"

"At least another full day's journey—maybe longer, dependin' on the wind. Don't you worry, I got lots more stories. It's nice to have someone besides Owl to tell them to." Gabriel tried not to let out a sigh at the prospect of more stories and decided to try once again to obtain information from Brishen.

"Why don't you tell me a story about your sister?"

"Why would you want to hear about her, when I could tell you about the time I met a one-legged troll hidin' in a journeyman's pushcart?"

"I'm sure that story is fascinating and I'd love to hear it...later, but really couldn't you tell me a little bit more about the Gypsy."

Brishen let out a loud laugh, "You're certainly a polite one—you lasted far longer than most people do listenin' to my tales. And I can see how impatient you are to know more about my sister." Brishen raised his eyebrows and said in a mocking tone, "Yes, of course, friends that's what you are---if you're just friends then I'm a bat's uncle."

"Your sister was just being kind to me—really, she's a kind person."

Brishen let out a laugh. "She's kind enough to those she thinks are worthy of her kindness. My sister's not the saint you seem to think she is. She's swindled many a fool she thinks deserves to be separated from his gold."

"Really?"

"Gotta say, all the ones I know of deserved it."

"What do you mean?"

"I mean she picked people who were cruel, unkind, and generally a blight on the rest of the world. She took their gold—their valuables—whatever meant most to them and gave it to others who she felt deserved such thin's."

"Seems a bit risky to me. Didn't the people she swindled ever get angry?"

"Good question. As good as my sister is at givin' wise counsel is as poor as she is at takin' it. Yes, it's dangerous to cross powerful people who care nothin' for hurtin' others."

"Is that why she's in trouble?"

"I've said enough—more than I meant to. You're a sneaky one I'll give you that! You just might suit my sister after all. Now we got hours and hours ahead of us so I think it's time for that story about the troll…"

The bright day had dimmed to a dark night and Brishen had finally gone quiet. The only sound was the lapping of the waves against the boat. After an hour or so, Owl swooped down from his roost and gave a loud hoot. Just beyond the horizon dark clouds spread across the sky.

"Looks like there's a storm comin'. Hold tight Gabriel! Lower the sails! Secure the riggings!"

The water grew choppy, heaving the boat roughly from side to side. The ship followed Brishen's commands while Gabriel grabbed onto the side, trying desperately not to lose his balance and tumble into the angry sea.

Gripping the helm tightly in his hands, Brishen tried with all his strength to turn the ship around. "I'll be an elephant's knees! There's no turnin' back now! We'll have to ride it out! Stand firm!"

The wind screamed around the ship, while Brishen held tightly to the wheel. A huge wave crashed over the ship and salt water cascaded over the two men. Owl flew frantically from one end of the ship to the other. Lightning split the sky and thunder shook the air. Heavy rain poured out from the darkened sky.

"You won't take me!" screamed Brishen at the sea. Another huge wave crashed over the ship, causing more cold water to wash over them. "I'll not surrender!" he screamed, even louder. There was a blinding light and a loud crash, the smell of wood burning.

"Lightning's struck the ship!" screamed Gabriel. "Brishen! Are you all right? We have to abandon ship!"

"Never! I can never leave my ship!"

The smoke became deeper and even the heavy rain couldn't put out the fire that was growing. Gabriel held his breath trying to get closer to Brishen. "This is madness! You can get another ship! You only have one life!" A large creaking sound filled the air. The mast was falling. "Look out!" screamed Gabriel. It fell toward Brishen knocking him into the waves. "No!" Gabriel screamed and jumped after him into the churning sea.

Sebastian awoke to darkness. He had slept for hours and now the bright sky had turned to a dark purple scattered with stars. The ghostly light of the crescent moon illuminated a path just beyond the well. Feeling stronger and more confident after his triumph over the dragon he started down the path, repeating the Swamp Witch's rhyme:

> *Down a path of broken stones,*
> *past a well that's filled with bones,*
> *hidden by thorny trees,*
> *there a ruined castle be.*
> *Across its moat and in its tower,*
> *you'll find the one who has the power.*

The path was filled with old rocks and dead branches, and appeared as though it hadn't been traveled in years. It wound round and round a steep hill. Continuing along, Sebastian was determined to find the ruined castle and the mysterious one who could help him.

Once he reached the top of the hill, Sebastian spotted some odd shadows ahead. Carefully, he moved
closer and discovered an archway made of thorny
trees. The moonlight cascading through their twisted
limbs made snake-like figures on the ground. They
formed a tunnel that stretched into a deep, gray fog.
Sebastian moved closer and heard rustling coming
from all directions. He took a step forward and the
rustling became louder and began to sound like the
murmuring of words.

"Ccc..aaa..sssss…aaaarrrrr..aaaa…iisssssss…casss
…aarrrrr…aaaiiissss."

With each step he took the sounds became clearer,
changing from syllables to words. "*Cas ar ais?*" he repeated allowed. "Turn back? Why should I turn back?"
A loud crackling came from behind and he spun
around. The opening he had come through had now
closed off. The trees' tiny thorns grew until they were
as curved and sharp as fish hooks. The trees inched
closer and closer to him, their whispers echoing "*Cas
ar ais…Cas ar ais..*"

Sebastian didn't move—didn't even blink. Standing
as still as possible, he said, "*Tobann roses mórathrú.*"
Quickly the thorns began to change. Their sharp claws
bloomed into blood red roses, their thick scent per-
fuming the foggy air. In a deeper voice, Sebastian
spoke again, "*Meath.*" The edges of the beautiful flow-

ers grew dark and black. Slowly, they withered, each one turning dark as charcoal; their petals crinkling, then crumbling like dust. The limbs that held them shriveled and in moments all that remained were piles of black dust.

"*Thoghairm gaoithe,*" Sebastian bellowed. A fierce wind blew, spinning the dust away and clearing a path amidst the fog. Continuing forward, he spotted something large ahead of him. "*Thoghairm dóiteáin.*" The familiar blue light grew from the palm of his hand and he raised it up for a closer look.

Ahead of him was a crumbling stone sign attached to a gnarled tree trunk that was more than three times Sebastian's size. Raising his light a bit higher, he translated the faded inscription.

"To cross beyond this mark
And travel to the deepest dark
You must forgo what matters most
Then be prepared to meet your ghost."

Sebastian closed his palm and extinguished the blue light. *Ghost?* he thought. *Ghosts are just fodder for foolish tales. When people die, they don't come back. They don't do anything. I learned that long ago.*

Sebastian could feel his body growing tired after his spells and slowly sank to the ground next to the sign.

He knew it was useless to fight the coming exhaustion. *Why must I be so weak?* Sebastian shut his eyes and fell into an untroubled slumber, while all around him the fog began to grow.

Gabriel clutched Brishen to him, struggling to keep both their heads above water. The wind was like a hungry wolf, howling and biting at them. Rain slashed across their faces, stinging Gabriel and blurring his vision. Lightning split open the sky and thunder roared so loudly, it was as though a giant were shouting in Gabriel's ears. Muscles straining, he swam away from the burning ship, trying to get them both far from the wreckage. Brishen's limp body felt as heavy as an iron anchor and Gabriel struggled to keep it from pulling him to the depths.

Waves smashed into them, and still Gabriel kept going, all the while gasping for air. His legs ached, his arms felt as though they were going to split open, but he was determined the two of them would survive. On and on, he swam toward the lone shadow of an bject he'd seen illuminated by the lightning.

Gabriel's thoughts were on salvation and he prayed that it was a boat in the distance, one that could save them both. But the closer Gabriel swam to the object, the clearer it became that it was not a ship, but rather a large piece of wood left from another boat's unfortunate demise. With very little strength remaining, Gabriel pulled Brishen onto the floating debris and hoisted himself up. The winds were dying down and the rain stopped. Exhaustion set in and Gabriel slipped into unconsciousness.

"Hey feller!" A voice called out waking Gabriel. "You 'live out there?"

"Yes, we are," Gabriel called out, his voice hoarse.

"We? There's just you." Gabriel opened his eyes wide and saw that Brishen was gone. He turned to see an old fisherman in a tiny wooden boat. Floating all around him was debris from the ship.

"Brishen was here! You didn't see him!"

"Sorry—there was only you. Sure someone was with you?"

"Yes—I saved him—when he fell from the ship—it was on fire—he was here," Gabriel's voice was urgent and unsteady. He rubbed his hand over his eyes and ignored the weakness he felt in his body. "Did you see an owl anywhere—a golden one?" The fisherman reached down and offered his hand to Gabriel and helped him onto the boat.

"A golden owl? Sorry son, I haven'a seen one of those 'round here in years."

"You're sure you haven't seen anyone else?" asked Gabriel, his voice so hoarse it was barely even a whisper.

"Not a soul. 'Fraid to say it looks like yer friend didn't make it—it's a terrible thing to lose a shipmate. I'm sure you did everythin' you could to help 'im. Some people you jus' canna save—doesna' matter if yer brave or good or strong. No stoppin' death. You jus' never know when the sky's gonna get angry and pluck you right outta yer life." The fisherman shook his head. "That was a hell of a storm last night. I ain't ne'er seen one like it 'fore and I've been fishin' these waters longer than you've been alive. Had the look of witchcraft about it. T'is a miracle you made it through alive."

A miracle? What kind of miracle lets me live and Brishen die? Gabriel stared out at the sea, watching the last remnants of the once beautiful ship float in the water. He wondered what Brishen's last moments had been like. *Was he in pain? Was he even aware of what was happening? Did it hurt?* Guilt swamped his heart.

As the fishing boat took him away, he watched the sunlight shimmer on the waves and saw a small wooden object floating in the water. It was the peacock feather he'd carved on deck. He reached down and felt the cool water splash his hand. He scooped it up and held it tight in the palm of his hand. "Oh Gypsy," he whispered. "Forgive me. It's my fault there's nobody left in the world who remembers your name."

"The sailor isn't *really* dead?" asked Casper, as Mrs. Kinder placed a porcelain bowl full of goulash in front of him.

"It certainly seems that way." Mrs. Kinder replied, as she put another bowl in front of Johanna.

"I thought you liked killing and fighting?" said Johanna.

"It's not the same. There wasn't a reason. Brishen had a magic ship! It just shouldn't end that way."

Mrs. Kinder put a basket of bread on the table and a bowl of goulash in front of her seat. The golden book was tucked snugly in the front pocket of her apron. "Well Casper, not all endings are going to be happy— or neat, or even fair. That's just the way life is." said Mrs. Kinder.

"Why couldn't Gabriel save him?" Johanna asked suddenly, her voice sounding oddly harsh.

Mrs. Kinder lifted her spoon and pointed at Johanna with it as she talked. "I've been around a long time and after all these years it seems to me that some people can be saved and some can't. I've found though, most of the time, things turn out just as they should," Mrs. Kinder answered in a steady voice.

"I don't see why Brishen *should* die," Casper argued. "Seems pointless, and..and stupid!"

"Well Casper, you're certainly entitled to your opinion—it won't change the story mind you, but you're most welcome to feel that way. Now how about we all have some dinner?" Mrs. Kinder responded.

Casper stared down at the reddish-brown mush in his bowl and gulped.

"It's an old family recipe—you'll love it," said Mrs. Kinder.

"Why doesn't Johanna try it first, since she was soooo good with the chopping?"

"Fine," Johanna said, wrinkling her nose at Casper. Gingerly, she picked up the spoon and scooped a bit up. She took a deep breath and tasted it, then started coughing and gasping. "I—I can't breathe. I need help!"

"Oh my god! You poisoned her! You're trying to kill her!" Casper screamed jumping from his seat.

Johanna burst out laughing. "You're such an idiot, Casper. Mrs. Kinder the goulash is delicious."

Casper's eyes narrowed and he sat back down in his chair. "You won't know when or how, but I will get you." He looked down in his bowl and pushed his spoon in. "And if this kills me, I'll come back from the grave to get you. So either way, you're toast." Casper finally took a taste.

Mrs. Kinder laughed. "Ah Casper, you tasted the goulash and still remain with the living."

"For now," Casper mumbled.

"So Casper, think you can handle another little scare?" asked Mrs. Kinder, a bit mischievously.

Casper's eyes narrowed again. "What *kind* of scare?"

"You'll just have to listen to the rest of the story to find out," answered Mrs. Kinder.

"Great! Scary stories are so much fun," Johanna answered.

Mrs. Kinder pulled the book from her apron and pushed her chair back a bit. Once again she angled the book away from the children so that they couldn't see what was written on the pages. "So let's get to it then…"

Sebastian woke up cold, his bones aching from the chill that permeated the air. He opened his eyes and the world was gray. Everything was covered in a fog so thick he couldn't see a single thing--no shapes, no structures, not even the sign he'd read before falling asleep. He placed his palm out in front of him, and it disappeared into the mist. When Sebastian opened his mouth to speak the familiar words that would create light, no sound came out. He tried again, but not so much as a hoarse whisper rose from his throat. His voice was gone.

Sebastian concentrated and repeated the words in his mind, "*Thoghairm dóiteáin.*" Still, there was no flame. Panic crawled inside Sebastian, making his heart beat faster. *I've done this before—this spell will work. It must!!* But as Sebastian tried to concentrate, doubt clouded his mind. He tried again and again, but still there was no flame. For the first time since he'd began travelling the world as a sorcerer, true terror crept into his heart.

Do I turn back? Can I turn back? Sebastian stood and stretched his hands out in front of him. Reaching into his cloak pocket, he grasped the stolen chisel. He held it out in a helpless attempt to ward off any creature that might attack and inched forward. A furious wind began to blow. With each step, the wind grew stronger. Sebastian shielded his eyes with his arm and tried to steady himself. The fog around him swirled, then parted to form a tunnel. Sebastian continued forward until he came to an old wooden drawbridge. It stretched across a moat whose waters were hidden by dark mists. The air was oddly silent. Even the wind that moved the fog had no sound. Everything was as voiceless as Sebastian.

As most drawbridges do, this one led to an enormous castle. Made of stone the color of raven feathers, the castle had a single square tower pierced with arched stained glass windows whose light shimmered a deep, blood red. The top of the tower disappeared completely in the fog, making the castle seem as if it had no end.

On the other side of the drawbridge were the castle's iron gates. They stood ominously shut. Sebastian walked forward. When his feet touched the drawbridge, the wood gave a shrill whine. Sebastian took several steps toward the middle of the bridge, when a plank bent under his weight. He began to run.

Beneath his feet, a rotten board broke with a loud crunch. His leg crashed through the opening and the wood tore his pants and scraped his skin.

Sebastian struggled to escape. The sound of rattling chains echoed in the fog. As he looked for the source of the sound, the drawbridge began to move. The chisel fell from his hand and skidded down the slope of the bridge until it clanked against the entry gates. Sebastian's struggling had no effect on the drawbridge, and it continued its steady rise.

As the drawbridge rose to a steep angle, Sebastian managed to wrench himself free. He slid down, tumbling over himself and banging into the gates with a crash. A rush of pain flared in his shoulders. But he ignored it and stood to face the gates. A large rusted lock held them in place.

"*Doras oscailte,*" he thought —but the lock did not budge.

Behind Sebastian the drawbridge kept moving. It was only a matter of moments until it would seal him into the narrow space between the stone archway and the gates. With a steady creak, it inched closer to him.

He turned to the bridge and in his mind, frantically shouted "*Stad!*" But once again his magic failed him and the bridge did not stop. Turning again, he stooped low to the ground and grabbed the chisel. Nearer and nearer the drawbridge moved. With a large rumble, it shut completely.

Sebastian was pinned between the iron gates and the wooden planks. He could not turn and if he tried to move forward or back, his clothes, and then his skin, would surely be torn by the bridge's rough wood or the gates' iron scrollwork. *This is what it must feel like to be inside a coffin*, he thought, and for just a moment the faces of the fisherman he'd sent to their graves flashed in his mind.

Sebastian concentrated on the words that should open the lock, *"Doras oscailte."* He repeated the phrase over and over in his mind. Still the lock didn't move.

He gripped the chisel in his hand and eased his arm toward the lock. Fiery pain ran through his body as the gates' metal scrollwork dug into his arm. Maneuvering the chisel into the lock's opening, Sebastian began to turn it. His breath came in shallow hiccups and sweat fell down his neck in cold drops. He twisted the chisel until his hands were rubbed raw and blood covered the handle. Finally, with a groan, the old metal lock opened and fell to the stone floor.

Sebastian pushed the gates open, coughing and gasping for air. Pausing for a moment to catch his breath, he shoved the chisel into his pocket. Wiping his bloody hands on his torn and stained cloak, he stepped into a long hallway lined with glowing torches and lifted one from the wall to light his way.

The hall ended in two towering stone doors. He raised his torch for a closer look and saw an iron door-knocker in the shape of an hourglass. Just above it was an inscription. He couldn't translate the symbols, but they were familiar. Where had he seen them before? The sound of a clanging bell and a crashing wave echoed in his ears. These were the same symbols inscribed on the box that had held his medallion! *Is this where my medallion came from?* Sebastian wondered. *Is there another somewhere inside?*

As so often is the case with people, his curiosity made him brave and without thought he pushed at the heavy doors. They didn't budge. He grasped the door-knocker, feeling the metal cold against his palm. He clanged it three times. The sound echoed off the stone walls and the doors rushed open. A powerful gust of wind swept him into the room beyond. Sebastian's eyes widened and his mouth formed a silent gasp.

He was in the center of an elaborate ballroom with a floor made of black and white stone squares and covered in layers of dust and dirt. Large spiders dangled from thick webs that coated an ornate chandelier. Perched around the outskirts of the ballroom were tall candelabras tarnished by time. Up a master staircase there was an empty throne. Like the chandelier, it was covered in cobwebs. On either side of the chair were two boarded up doors, and on the wall, there appeared to be a painting of some sort that was covered in a dirty cloth. Enormous, it spanned almost the length and height of the entire wall. But it was not the sight of these things that had shocked Sebastian, but rather what he saw in the large bronze mirrors that lined the walls.

He stared at the mirrors and instead of seeing a dark, cobweb filled space in the reflection, there was a lively ballroom. It seemed to be the same room, but the chandelier sparkled, the floors gleamed, and the candelabras were brightly lit with red candles. And the reflected ballroom was not empty. It was filled with dancing figures. The women wore glittering dresses that dripped with jewels and the men, immaculate suits interwoven with golden thread. Scores of couples spun round and round in a spirited waltz.

But instead of beautiful, smiling faces the dancers were gaunt and skeletal. They looked as though they had been people once, but had been left out in the sun too long and had shriveled like raisins. Abruptly they all stopped and turned to face Sebastian. In each of the hundred mirrors the terrible figures were reflected. Hundreds of ghastly faces all turned toward him, their sunken eyes watching him through glass.

They moved closer to the mirrors, stretching out their bony hands toward him. Horrified, Sebastian crawled backward to the center of the room. He watched with wide eyes, as one by one the figures stepped through the mirrors. Absolute terror pulsed through him. He had no magic—no escape—no hope. Sebastian opened his mouth to scream, but no sound came out. The only noise that filled the ballroom was the rustling of their silk and velvet clothes as they closed in around him.

6

OF MIRRORS AND MEMORIES

Gabriel looked around the fisherman's home. The furniture was simple and worn, consisting mostly of a battered table and mismatched stools. Drift wood was piled up near the entrance to the kitchen, where Gabriel could just see the edge of the wood burning stove. There were fishing nets to be mended piled in a corner and fish traps hanging from the low ceiling. Everything was just as Gabriel would expect in the home of a fisherman. Except for the walls.

Sprouting over all the walls were perfectly painted tree branches with almond shaped leaves. Peering out from some of the leaf edges were tiny bluebirds. Nor-

mally Gabriel would have been fascinated by the intricate artwork, and wondered who the artist was and
why he'd chosen to paint this picture, but instead he
looked away.

"I've been tellin' 'im how yer fish stew's the best in
the village." The fisherman called to his wife.

"In the village! It's the best in the whole Ambrian
coast!" A short woman with kind blue eyes framed by
wrinkles emerged from the kitchen. She wiped her
hands on her bright patchwork apron. Her voice
sounded surprisingly young. "At least, that was what
the Cobbler told me when he asked me ta run off with
'im."

"You always tell that same story 'bout that foolish
old goat. Iffen the Cobbler's so pleasin' ta you, why
didn't you run off with 'im!"

The fisherman's wife gave her husband a smile.
"Yer an old fool iffen you think I'd run off with some
man, just cause he fell in love with my stew. Phineaus,
if I didn't know any better I'd say you were raised with
pigs, since yer guest 'as been standin' here without so
much as a 'how do you do'."

"Always naggin', she is. Suppose I should give you a
formal introduction-else I'll ne'er hear the end of it.
Gabriel—this here's Matilda—my Tilly--the love o' my
life—even if she'll nag me 'til my bones are buzzard
food. Darlin, Gabriel here lost his ship in that storm

last night. I thought we could 'elp 'im out fer the night."

Tilly took in Gabriel's damp clothes, scraped hands and haggard appearance and her voice softened. "Poor dear, you look like you lost a battle with a sea dragon. After the look a' last night's storm, I think you mighta had better luck with a sea dragon. Whalebones! I've been jabberin' on so, when you must be starvin'. We best get you out of those wet things and I'll fix you a nice bowl o' hot stew. You need some meat on those bones--yer practic'lly a skeleton."

Tilly rummaged through an old chest and handed Gabriel some breeches, socks, and a shirt. They were too large to belong to Phineaus, which made Gabriel wonder whose they'd been.

While Gabriel changed, Tilly poured steaming stew into copper bowls and set a loaf of thick crusty bread on the table. When Gabriel joined the couple, Tilly exclaimed, "Now you eat every last bite, you hear. You'll need it to build yer strength!" They ate together in silence while she watched as Gabriel swallowed spoonful after spoonful, then in a voice both rough and tender, ordered him to sit by the fire to "warm his bones." He mumbled out a thank you to them both and went over to the hearth.

Gabriel sat gazing into the flames. Not quite sadness, not quite loneliness, but something entirely different had taken root inside him; as if a storm cloud had found its way into his heart and was eclipsing any sunlight. He heard the clanking of pots as Tilly tidied the kitchen and then her voice rang out, surprisingly clear and sweet.

> *"So many kinds of birds there be,*
> *That fly along the land and sea,*
> *Larks and doves and even 'gales,*
> *And golden ones with silver tails.*
> *But there be only one that nests*
> *Inside the leaves of happiness."*

Gabriel felt a stab inside his chest, like the edges of wood that's been splintered by an ax. He listened to the notes and in his mind heard his mother's lullaby, soft and low. He could feel her tender touch against his cheek. It was replaced by the rough warmth of his grandfather's hands as they moved over his own while they carved a rose together. Then the hands became soft and delicate—the touch of the Gypsy. Her mesmerizing eyes gazed at him and her mysterious smile changed into Brishen's laughing grin.

Gone, he thought. *Everyone's gone.* The stabbing inside Gabriel changed to a deep ache, like the way his muscles felt after he'd spent hours carving. He felt anger trickle through, like water into broken rock. It spilled into the cracks in his heart, making it feel as heavy as stone. *What use is it to care, if you lose it all? What's the point? I've failed everyone—the ice maiden, Brishen, the Gypsy.* The hands that rested on his thighs turned into fists.

"Feelin' better?" Phineaus asked, taking a seat in the wood chair next to Gabriel. He held a pipe tight in his weathered hand. Tilly sat at the kitchen table knitting, the sound of the needles clinking echoed in the shanty.

Gabriel let his hands uncurl, and suddenly felt tired. "No." It had taken great effort for him to answer.

"You should be, that was some storm you survived. I'm sure yer friend would be 'appy that you made it."

"He's dead. I doubt he can be happy about anything—or sad for that matter." Sharpness edged Gabriel's voice.

"You sure 'bout that?"

"I haven't spoken with any dead people lately, but I'm pretty certain."

"No, doesn't seem like you have. The dead can talk ta you—if yer willin' ta listen. Maybe you just haven'a been payin' attention."

An odd laugh came out of Gabriel, harsh and tinny.

Phineaus leaned back and lit his pipe, its warm scent wafted through the cabin. The smell reminded Gabriel of something he couldn't quite remember.

"Ya know there's a sayin' 'mong us fishing folk. Survive a storm like that and yer marked by the winds."

"The winds?"

"You know, the winds. What's the fancy word for it? Destiny—that's it. The winds have a plan in mind fer you. Great or terrible, no one can say, but somethin' special that's fer sure."

"Just because I survived a storm?"

"No," Phineaus shook his head, "Cause you survived a storm like that and no one survives that kinda storm without a good reason."

"If you ask me there doesn't seem to be much of a reason for anything."

Phineaus looked into Gabriel's eyes, "I think a feller like you knows better than that."

"That's where you're wrong." Gabriel let out a disgusted sound. "I'm not marked by the winds, or anything else! I'm just a sculptor who got tangled up in some magic. I'm no more important or powerful than anyone else."

"You part of some big magic?"

"All I did was make a statue one night—that's it. No spells, no storms, nothing."

"Sounds like the beginnin' of a story—iffen I've e'er heard one. And it sounds like it's a tale you have a need ta tell."

"There's nothing to tell."

"Funny thing with painful stories—hold 'em in and they eat at you—jus' like a hungry dog with a bone. Too much of that can make a man hard. Think real careful if that's a road you want ta be travelin' down. It's long and cold, and I known many a good soul lost their way 'long it."

"What is telling you going to accomplish?"

"Well, what's not tellin' it doin' fer you? 'Sides maybe I can help you somehow."

"The last person who tried to help me ended up at the bottom of the sea. You sure you want to volunteer?" Gabriel responded, looking into Phineaus' eyes.

"The winds brought you to my door, so fer good or not yer story's one I'm s'posed to hear."

"Have you ever seen an angel?" Gabriel asked. "I did. She was in there—just asking me to let her out. What choice did I have?" He told Phineaus the entire tale, beginning with the moment he'd first seen the ice maiden. He spoke of his travels and how the Gypsy had helped him even when he'd lost all hope. "For almost as long as I can remember, I've been on my own. She was the first person who made me feel like I wasn't alone in the world, that life could be warm and full."

Tilly kept knitting, but listened carefully and every so often her gaze moved to Gabriel's face. While Gabriel spoke of his journey with Brishen, Phineaus raised his pipe and breathed in deeply. Slowly he exhaled and the smoke made delicate curls in the air.

"He made me laugh and he was very brave," Gabriel said, finishing his story. "How can the Gypsy ever forgive me for letting her brother die?" Gabriel put his head in his hands.

"I'm sure she knows it's not yer fault, even iffen you don't. Didn't you say she's the one that sent you on that ship?"

"Yes, to see a goblin. I'm supposed to find some kind of relic, something that's powerful and cursed—something strong enough to bring the ice maiden to life. The Gypsy should have known I couldn't do this! Whatever it is I'm searching for probably made that storm. I make statues, not magic—I'm not cut out for this."

Phineaus' eyes took on a somber light. He put down his pipe, his hands trembling.   "Did she tell you anything 'bout what yer looking for?"

"Just that it's a powerful and dangerous charm."

"Same could be said fer many thin's," said Phineaus, his voice taking on a nervous twinge.

"She told me that people believe that wherever there's been a disaster, it's been there first."

"It canna be." Panic flashed in Phineaus' face.

"Finney, might not be what ya think it t'is," Tilly said gently.

"Of course it t'is! That's what brought 'im 'ere," shouted Phineaus. He turned to Gabriel. "You must forget 'bout it!" he said. "T'is too dangerous, boy!"

"But you said I was 'marked by the winds'."

"Them's just fishfolk rubbish—means nothin'."

Gabriel grabbed his arm. "You know something—you have to tell me, after everything that's happened!"

"I tell you, I don't know nothin'!" Phineaus shook off Gabriel's hold and stood up to leave. "I needs air." He called out to his wife, "'Tilly, I'm goin' fer a bit of a walk."

Tilly looked at him with concern, but her voice was calm and even. "Jus' be sure to come back in, iffen it looks like it's gonna rain."

Gabriel turned to her. "He knows something! And you do too. You have to tell me!"

Tilly stood up, leaving her knitting on the table and sat in the chair her husband had vacated.

"What yer talkin' 'bout might not even be the same thing that's on his mind."

"What does he think it is?"

She took a deep breath. "You told yer story—and a pretty hard one t'was to tell. Only seems fair, I tell you a hard one too. There was a charm, a very old, magic charm. They say a pirate Cap'n found it—no one knows exactly where. There's lots of diff'rent stories. Some say he stole it from a castle after he killed everyone who lived there. 'Nother story said he slayed a sea witch who wore it 'round her neck. No one knew where it came from and far as I know no one does. That old Pirate paid a conjurer a king's ransom to put some spells on it, so it'd be safe when he went ma-raudin'."

"Why didn't he just take it with him?"

"Too dangerous. Even the Pirate knew havin' it on board would curse his ship. He used to stop in this vil-lage from time to time; figured it was a quiet enough place where the charm would be safe. He kep' it up in the old church tower with whatever spells that con-juror put on it. Don't know if it was just people talkin', or the magic in that charm, but word that there was hidden treasure here spread out like fog 'cross the sea. That old charm drew people in as though it was water and they were all dyin' of thirst. One by one people kep' tryin' to get up in that tower, each thinkin' there was some wonderful treasure beyond imaginin' just waitin' for them." Her voice grew shaky. The firelight was reflected in the tears that sparkled in the corners of her eyes. "Even the kindest people were drawn to it. That charm turned 'em all into greedy fools. One by one, disaster found 'em—the closer they came to suc-ceedin', the more terrible their fate. Not a soul knew what became of the Pirate—he never came back and no one heard from 'im again. So many years went by people forgot about even tryin' ta steal it—was as impossible as tryin' ta touch the moon." She paused again, taking another deep breath, her hand clutching the front of her apron.

"Til one night, 'bout three years ago, a stranger snuck into town. Townfolk say it were some kind of monster pretendin' to be a boy. He must have been too, since he managed to snatch up that charm without so much as ne'er you mind. After he'd got his hands on it, that old bell rang out and tons of menfolk came running outta their houses, thinkin' the old Pirate had returned and maybe they could snatch up the treasure for themselves. A big group of 'em cornered the boy." Her hands began to tremble. "No one's sure whether it was that strange boy or that terrible charm, but the ocean came right up and swallowed all those men. In one big wave, all of 'em were gone." Tilly stared into the fire.

"We lost so much that day. T's a hard story for us to tell, that's why old Finney couldn't bear to talk 'bout it. Our son was at the dock that night. Jus' like all the others, he was washed away. He was a good boy—such a good boy, kind and sweet, always wantin' to help, always sayin' somethin' sweet 'bout how nice supper was, or how fine the sweater I'd made him was. He painted all those branches and birds. He had a way with 'em. Birds would just fly up to him and perch on his shoulders. He said he wanted to paint me a little bit o' happiness." Tilly wiped tears from her eyes. "Every day, I look at those birds and 'member how happy he was when he painted 'em."

Gabriel reached out and put his hand over hers.

"Yer a good boy too. And I'm 'fraid for you. I'd tell you to give up, but my husband's right—you've been marked by the winds and you must do what you must. But, I've got hope fer you. In my heart, I know you'll stop this charm from hurtin' anyone else."

"What makes you think that? I'm just trying to take it for my own selfish reasons just like all the others."

She gave his hand a warm squeeze. "Not alike at all. Yer lookin' for it cause yer heart is so full of love, it won't let you rest 'til you set things right."

"Love?"

"Of course, my boy, in the end that's what all great journeys are about, in one way or 'nother. There's greatness ahead of you, even an old woman like me can see that."

Gabriel gave Tilly a warm kiss on the cheek. "Thank you for your kindness, for everything. I should leave tomorrow—I have to go on. I'm going to find that goblin. The Gypsy thought he could help me and I must trust her."

Tilly nodded. "You'll find yer way." She touched his cheek softly. "Now get to bed, you'll need yer rest. Sweet dreams."

"Good night," answered Gabriel with a nod. Those were the last words spoken in the cabin that night. Tilly went to bed and Phineaus returned hours later to join her, while Gabriel lay on floor with his wool blanket tucked around him. In silence, he watched the flames dance, until his eyes shut and all was darkness.

Sebastian searched for an escape route from the ballroom, but the ominous figures surrounded him on all sides. Their cold, hard fingers twined around his limbs. Whenever they touched him, a deep chill spread through his body, like his bones had been dipped in ice water and were now frozen. His panic and horror shifted to an icy calmness. His heartbeat slowed its frantic pace and an odd sort of peacefulness filled his mind. The ghastly figures pulled him up to stand. As he stared at their emaciated faces, they no longer seemed grotesque. There was a strange beauty to them now, like dead flowers. When the hint of a spring blossom glimmers through the decay.

One by one the figures walked toward the mirrors and crossed the threshold. Like a fish stuck on a hook, Sebastian had no choice but to move where they pulled him. There was no argument in his mind—no struggle in his soul. The only desire left inside him was the impulse to follow. And so, he walked toward one of the bronze mirrors and stepped through.

Sebastian felt a frigid gust of air and a sensation like falling. Colors swirled around him and in a moment he was in the glittering ballroom. Filling his nostrils was the scent of flowers, wine, and sweet cakes. Filling his ears was a lively and cheerful minuet. The figures turned away from Sebastian and began to dance once more. All around him they spun.

Sebastian turned to face the master staircase and its golden throne. He felt his will returning to him and began to remember why he had come to this castle in the first place. He moved up the stairs and toward the painting. On this side of the mirror, the painting was covered in golden brocade. Sebastian couldn't fight the sudden desire to see what was hidden behind the cloth.

He reached the top of the stairs and stood in front of the painting. Grabbing the heavy fabric, he felt it stiff and scratchy against his sore hands. Sebastian pulled. It fell to the floor revealing a painting of a large spiral staircase.

A vague sense of disappointment flooded Sebastian. He had not known what to expect, but this seemed so ordinary. Sebastian moved his face closer to see if he had missed anything and reached up to touch the paint. It felt wet against his fingers and when he pulled back there was paint on his hand. *It doesn't look wet,* he thought. *What kind of magic is this?*

As if in response to Sebastian's thoughts, the colors of the painting began to run. They poured from the frame like a waterfall and splashed over him. The liquid smelled foul, like dirt and swamp. He tried to back away, but bumped into the back of the golden throne. More and more liquid poured from the painting oozing onto the floor and splashing over everything. Suddenly a giant wave came crashing through the painting, washing over Sebastian's head. The liquid was heavier than water; heavier than paint. Sebastian felt as like he was being encased in stone. In that moment, he was sure his journey was over and he had failed.

Sebastian opened his eyes. Whether minutes, days, or years had passed he could not tell. He found himself at the bottom of a spiral staircase like the one in the painting. Somehow, he'd made his way inside the picture. It was dark and eerily quiet, the kind of sound that either precedes, or follows something terrible.

He looked around but there were no doorways or pictures, no way in or out, except the lone staircase that spiraled upward. The voice of the Swamp Witch reached through the confusion in his mind— *in its tower, you'll find the one who has the power....* It seemed a lifetime ago that she'd spoken the words that sent him on this quest.

Sebastian tried to speak—to utter some words of protection, but still no sound escaped his lips. He steadied himself and climbed the stairs. They stretched out for what seemed like miles and so he kept climbing, all the time expecting something monstrous to jump out from the shadows. He made it to the top landing, which was empty, save for a long, gilded mirror hanging on the stone wall. Moving closer, Sebastian saw his reflection.

His dark hair had grown long and ragged. His face was covered with cuts and scrapes and his blue eyes were rimmed with red. As he stared in the mirror, he could barely recognize himself. Sebastian was disgusted at the image staring back at him. He looked weak and tired. He was a powerful sorcerer! Not a weak and frail mortal. A flush of angry determination replaced the shame. He had made it this far and would not turn back. Failure was a choice and not one he would make. He would finish this journey.

Sebastian placed his hand against the mirror and the glass melted like smoke. He stepped across the frame and found himself in a room made entirely of mirrors. There were endless images of himself, reflecting from every surface. Behind each one was another, each one moving as he did.

Suddenly, he wasn't the only object being reflected. There was a dark shadow-- black as pure emptiness. Slowly, it inched closer until it filled all the mirrors: a black robed figure with no face and no eyes. It stared out at Sebastian from all sides—the floor, the ceiling, the walls—everywhere the empty face watched.

I've been waiting for you. The words echoed in the Sorcerer's head. They were not formed by a sound in the room, but materialized inside his mind. The voice wasn't human, nor like any magical creature he had ever encountered. It was a sound that had no sound at all. Though Sebastian struggled to remain calm, his body still trembled at the unearthly presence. *I know why you've come.*

So, you'll help me? asked Sebastian silently in his mind.

I am not here to help you, or harm you. You were in possession of something which belongs to me. It sought you out and yet here you are and it is elsewhere.

The medallion?

That is what you call it. It is known by many names. It is a dangerous object for a mere mortal. Had it not chosen you, finding it would have meant your destruction.

Why did it choose me?

Because the medallion seeks out those who most desire what it has to give.

Destruction? asked Sebastian, thinking of that terrible wave and the drowning fishermen.

Yes. But within that power lays another. There is a balance in this world and the medallion seeks to maintain it. It destroys, but by the same token it can create. It was drawn to you because of your desire for one of those two aims.

But I gave it to the Swamp Witch! She wouldn't tell me how to find you otherwise.

Ah, yes, I am aware. A cunning creature she is. She has sent you to me, when all along you carried the very thing you needed to fulfill your wish.

What! screamed Sebastian in his mind. *That sneaky, traitorous—*

The voice abruptly cut off the internal tirade. *As I said, the medallion can both create and destroy. It sought you out because of your desire for destruction and now it seeks another for the opposite purpose.*

The Swamp Witch?

No, she is merely holding it. She has not the ability to use it. As with the knowledge she guards, she revels in possessing the rare and unique.

So who is the medallion seeking ? How can I get it back?

The medallion has a will of its own—it will search for balance and will not detour from its chosen path. As for whom it seeks, I cannot say. Just that there is another soul who can wield its power.

You must help me! I must get it back! I must bring her to life!

All the power you need, you already possess. I will let you leave from here, on the condition that should the medallion choose you, you will return it to me. This is not a request. Should you fail to comply no amount of magic will spare your fate.

You have my word that once I've used it to bring the maiden to life, I will return it to you. But please, tell me who is this 'other' the medallion seeks?

With that, all the mirrors around Sebastian shattered. With a loud crash, the mirror floor beneath his feet cracked and gave way. He was falling into empty darkness and landed abruptly. He was now sitting on the throne in the cob-web filled ballroom. The mirrors that surrounded the outskirts of the room were broken.

Sebastian ran from the ballroom, through the now open castle gates and across the drawbridge, into the bright sun. He dusted himself off and looked down at his hands. Miraculously his cuts and scrapes had vanished. He no longer felt weak and sore. Sebastian tested his voice. "*Thoghairm beag dóiteáin.*" A small blue flame spiraled from his palm. He quickly extinguished it. His powers had returned and now he was ready. He knew what he had to do.

After several plates of eggs, kippers and biscuits, along with two full bowls of porridge, it was finally time for Gabriel to leave the shanty. Golden sunlight pushed through the doorway behind Phineaus and Tilly, as they stood waiting to give Gabriel their good-byes.

"You promise me ya'll be careful now," said Tilly as she rubbed her hands against her apron. "You don' do nothin' foolish. And don' forget what I told you." She paused a moment and stared at Gabriel's face, trying to keep the details etched in her mind, so on cold winter nights when she told Gabriel's story she could perfectly describe the kindness and courage and sadness she saw gleaming inside him. "I packed this sack fer you, it's got some food, clothes and a warm blanket." She handed him a small leather bag.

"I really can't accept any more of your kindness— "

"Now, doncha start in with that foolishness. Does an old woman's heart good ta have a young one ta fuss over."

"My darlin's never so happy as when she's taking care of someone—so dontcha go spoilin' it," said Phineaus with a wink.

Gabriel gave a laugh, "I should have known better than to argue with either of you. You have been so generous to me. I have something for you—it's not much, but I couldn't think of anything else to give." Gabriel pulled an object from the pocket of his breeches. Sitting on his palm was a carved bluebird. He offered it to the Tilly. "This is for you." Tears shimmered in her eyes. Phineaus put a steady hand on her shoulder.

"Isna that just the most perfect thing ya ever seen, sweetheart?" Tilly paused for a moment then continued, "So precious." She reached out and ran her hand over the wood. "How did you—when— "

Gabriel coughed back the lump that had formed in his throat while he had watched the emotion fill her face. "Before you woke up, I used a piece of firewood and a kitchen knife. I didn't have my tools or I'd have done a better job—"

"No, no! It's perfect—so perfect. Perfect little bit o' happiness. I'll keep it forever." She picked up the bird and clutched it to her chest and threw her arms around Gabriel. "You're a good boy, such a good boy to bring a little light inta an old woman's life—and I'll 'member you always." Gabriel felt a squeezing in his heart.

"I could never forget either of you."

Phineaus clapped a firm hand on Gabriel's back.

Tilly pulled away from him and looked up into his face. In a firm voice, she said, "I know you got a long road 'head of you. It'll be hard and lonely and sometimes more scary than anythin' I could tell you about. But just 'member ta hold onto all the good and love that's inside you—iffen you do that, no matter how dark it gets you'll always find yer light."

"Thank you both so much— "

"--No need ta thank us, boy," answered Phineaus. "You brought back some 'appy memories ta us and them's worth more than gold. You be safe now and when all's said and done you come see us again."

"I will," answered Gabriel as he gave Phineaus a firm handshake.

"Jus' follow the path 'way from town that goes up inta the mountains. It'll be a bit steep but it'll take ya 'round, then down into the woods. If ya keep going 'ventually ya'll reach the frozen forest. Never made the journey meself so I'm not 'xactly sure which way ta tell you ta turn."

"That's more than enough, I'm sure I'll find my way."

"I know you will. Good journey m'boy and may the winds be with you all the way." Gabriel gave the couple a nod and left the shanty. He felt warm inside, like a stone that had sat in the sun and absorbed its heat. Gabriel had been cold, lonely and lost, and for a moment he remembered what it was like to have a family. Phineaus and Tilly believed in him, believed that this quest would make a difference—that there were good things he was supposed to do.

Maybe they're right, maybe there's more to my journey than death and sorrow, thought Gabriel.

And as he continued down the path and toward the rocky slope of mountain that stood at the edge of the fishing village, Gabriel was surprised to notice that despite everything he'd lost on this journey, he still had hope. He turned and glanced back one last time at the fishing village, then turned forward to begin his climb.

She tricked me. **She** *tricked* **me.** These words echoed over and over in Sebastian's mind as he journeyed first through the barren stretch of forest where he'd battled the dragon and onward into the lush woods that led away from the path. He imagined in vivid detail what he'd do to the Swamp Witch when he found her. First, he envisioned a spell where her long seaweed hair would twine itself around her neck, tighter and tighter 'til it choked the life right out of her. Then he thought of magic words that would make the swampy water where she lived grow hotter and hotter until it cooked her straight through, like an old fish in a bubbling stewpot. *No, no*, he thought. *She has my medallion and no simple spell will do. She tricked me and I'm going to have to do the same to get back what she stole from me.*

The night began to kiss the sky and the darkness was easing over the trees. Sebastian scouted a safe area and settled down to camp for the night at the foot of a massive oak tree. He sat on the soft earth and his hand brushed against some weeds on the ground. He grabbed a handful of dandelions and held the thin stems in his fingers. How long had it been since he'd seen one of these? A memory flooded Sebastian's mind.

"You'll never catch me!" she cried out, in a voice as sweet as a happy dream.

"You always say that and I always do," called a fifteen-year-old Sebastian as he chased the young woman through the woods. "*Titim síos,*" he whispered softly and the amber haired girl tripped, landing softly into a pile of leaves. He caught up to her and stood smirking at her prone form.

"Elise, how many times have I told you that you'll never outrun me?"

"You wouldn't have caught me if I wasn't so clumsy," Elise answered crossly. Then suddenly a smile slid across her lips and her eyes lit with excitement. "It looks as though I'm lucky as well as hopelessly clumsy—you never find these at this time of year." She clutched in her hand one dandelion with its tiny white sprouts in a perfect sphere.

"What do you mean lucky? That's just a weed—completely worthless—even warthogs won't eat them."

"Don't you know about these flowers?"

"Flowers? They're not flowers, just raggedy weeds."

"Always gloom and doom Sebastian, can't you ever see the possibilities in anything? This is a flower, even if it's not as obviously beautiful as the other kinds. But what's special about this one, is that it grants wishes."

"Wishes? Exactly how does a raggedy weed grant a wish, pray tell?"

"Come sit here. Don't argue with me—just sit," Elise answered. As usual, he gave in to her demand. Leaves crunched beneath Sebastian as he sat on the ground next to her. "My mother told me about dandelions—didn't your mother tell you?"

"My mother wasn't around to tell me anything. She ran off when I was a baby. That's what Malvina told me, anyway." *Over and over,* he thought. *She never stops telling me how worthless my mother was and how even more worthless I am.* Sebastian stared at the ground in front of him and pulled at a few stray blades of grass.

Tenderness crept into the Elise's voice, "Here now, take this one." When Sebastian felt her soft skin touch his as she placed the flower in his hand, his heart gave an odd sort of jump. "Close your eyes, and think of what you want—of the single thing you want more than anything else in the world. But under no circumstances can you tell me what it is—that would ruin it. Now open your eyes and blow all the seeds away."

He followed her instructions and let out a huge breath. The white seeds danced in the wind and scattered. "That's it?" he asked.

"That's it."

"And that's supposed to make my wish come true?"

"Of course," she replied and gave him a huge smile. "But only if you truly believe it. Things only have as much magic as you give them."

Sebastian's heart ached as he remembered Elise. She'd been his best friend—his *only* friend. He wished desperately not to think about that last time he'd seen her, but as so often is the case with painful memories, opening the door a crack to see one *little* thing, lets out a flood of others. And so, Sebastian began to remember.

A sixteen-year-old Sebastian stood silently at the edge of town, hiding behind some trees, and waiting for Elise. The moment she rounded the corner, a smile lit his face.

"Sebastian!" she called out, running to him.

Before Elise could say another word, Sebastian held out his hand and said, "Come with me." Grabbing Elise's hand tightly, he led her into the woods.

"Oh Sebastian, always so serious." Elise laughed. "Where are we going? Is this some kind of prank?"

"Shhh," he hushed her. "There's something important I need to talk to you about." He stopped when they'd reached a small stream surrounded by thick bushes. "I want you to come away with me. We have to get away from here."

"We?" Elise asked.

"Yes, it's not safe—"

"What do you mean?" Elise asked growing alarmed.

"My grandmother--Malvina, she knows I—I care about you. She'll hurt you." Sebastian continued urgently.

"I know she's a cruel woman, and she's treated you terribly, but there's no reason to think— "

"She's going to use you to hurt me. We must run away. We can leave together—I'll keep you safe, I promise."

"Sebastian you're overreacting— "

"No!" he shouted and grabbed Elise by the shoulders. "There's so much you don't know. She's dangerous—she'll hurt you. Please, for once, listen to me. We need to leave."

Elise looked at Sebastian and realized she'd never seen him so afraid. She held his hands within her own. "It'll be all right Sebastian. I'll go with you, wherever you want. I just need to stop home first. Grab a few things and leave a note for my parents—I don't want them to worry."

"It's dangerous, Elise— "

"I promise I'll meet you back here in two hours."

"I'm not sure— "

Elise squeezed his hands. "It will be all right. I promise."

"I should go with you," Sebastian argued.

"You know my parents don't approve of you. They'd never let me leave. Two hours won't make a difference at all. Just wait for me." She touched his cheek and gave him a sweet smile. "It'll be a wonderful adventure, like the kind we always talked about having—you'll see."

Sebastian waited and grew more anxious with each passing minute. He paced the bank of the small stream, back and forth—until two hours had long passed. The sun was sinking in the sky and soon it would be dark.

"Sebastian, dear boy." Sebastian whirled around and there stood the person he hated more than anyone else in the world. She looked old and feeble, with her deep wrinkles, wispy gray hair, and dark eyes, but her voice was hard as an iron sword. "You should have known you couldn't escape."

"Where is she! Tell me now!" Sebastian screamed.

Malvina let out a laugh. "Why the worry? She's just waiting for you back at our home."

Sebastian ran quickly through the darkness, while the woman's cackling laughter followed him. He made it to the shabby cottage where he lived with Malvina and threw open the door.

"No!" he screamed. Lying on the floor was Elise, crumpled and pale, her yellow dress pooled around her like a melting sun. Sebastian bent down and cradled her in his arms. He put his ear to her heart, checked for her breath—but there was nothing. Elise was so full of life, so sweet--so kind. She was all the warmth Sebastian had ever known. Now she was cold and still and empty—and worst of all, gone. He rocked her back and forth, and murmured every magical word that he knew.

"It's far too late for that now," that familiar and evil voice called from the doorway. "She's dead. And there's no magic you have that can bring her back. Now you'll do exactly what I tell you to— "

Sebastian turned to her, his eyes cold, his voice oddly steady. "How?" An emotion unlike any Sebastian had ever known burned hot in his belly.

Malvina laughed again. "She was quite easy to find and even easier to convince that I had only the best of intentions. Of course I loved my dear Sebastian and I was only hard on him because I wanted the very best for him. Then I asked her sweetly to come to our home so the two of us could have a nice chat over a cup of tea." She let out another dark laugh. "Her innocence was really quite charming. She had no reason to suspect the poison in her cup."

"Did you really think you'd get away Sebastian? Did you think you were some kind of hero?" Malvina sneered. "You? That's so sad. And I must say, a bit pathetic since you haven't figured out the most obvious part. You're a terrible boy—there's not a single thing about you that could ever resemble a hero. You'll never be the noble knight and rescue the fair maiden. You're the monster, the serpent, the dragon—the evil being that all those good men spend their lives trying to destroy. Where do you think your magic comes from? Did you think you just happened to find a spell book in the woods?" Malvina laughed. "I left it for you. Your destiny is to be evil and to use your magic to help me. Some people are good—like your little girl there, and that's what happens to good people. They believe the best and suffer terribly for it. You're like me, and you need to accept your fate."

"No!" Sebastian screamed and grabbed a knife from the table. There was no thought in Sebastian's mind, just anger and pain. He lunged through the air, with the knife raised above his head. With an angry thrust, he plunged into Malvina's chest. He tumbled over her as blood seeped from her wound and covered his hand.

Malvina let out one final laugh. "You see Sebastian, I was right. You are a monster—just like me." Malvina coughed out blood, then her head fell back and she was dead. Sebastian looked down at his blood-soaked hands and began to shake. Then he looked back at Elise—so very beautiful and so very still.

* * * *

"Enough!" the older Sebastian shouted aloud to himself, breaking out of his memory. Just thinking of that night left him shaking. That was when he'd run away—when he'd left that little village and never looked back. He stared at the dandelions in his hand. It had been so long since he'd thought of Elise. *She's gone*, Sebastian thought, *there's no point in thinking of her now.*

As he kept staring at the dandelion, he envisioned Elise's face and was suddenly filled with the urge to make a wish and scatter those seeds into the air. But he remembered clearly that wish he'd made years before, and how Elise was wrong. His dreams hadn't come true, instead they were only nightmares.

Instead, in a hollow voice he said, "*Mórathrú tobann le bia.*" The weeds grew dark and dry and transformed into long strips of meat jerky. Sebastian took a bite out of one and within a few moments had finished them all. He closed his eyes and tried to rest but despite having just filled his stomach, Sebastian felt decidedly empty. He forced himself to forget and tried to ignore that slow and steady pain that crept into his heart.

Gabriel followed the rocky path that wound its way up the mountain. It was steep, but quiet and all he could think about was his impending meeting with the goblin. What is a goblin really like? He'd heard so many stories about them. They were deformed and disgusting, and demanded all manner of valuables in exchange for the slightest favor. He'd even heard that if people tried to get out of paying them, they would steal their first born child, roast them over an open fire, and eat them—bones and all.

Gabriel couldn't imagine that this was true of the goblin—since the kind Gypsy had dealings with him, but still he was worried—particularly since he'd lost the peacock feather the Gypsy had given him. He had his carved wooden one and hoped it would be enough to satisfy the goblin.

As sunset dripped honey on the sky, Gabriel reached the top of the mountain. There were knobby pine trees, the remains of old campfires, and the bones of small animals that had fed hungry travelers who had passed this way.

Gabriel turned to view the path he'd climbed. The shanties of the fishing village dotted the coast like little white ducks on a rocky pond. Further out the light reflected on the waves and scattered sailboats moved across the horizon while seagulls dipped down to the kiss the water.

He turned to look ahead. There was another path leading down to the forest where lush green trees clustered together. Out into the distance the green turned to white and the frozen forest loomed. That was where he'd meet the goblin. And beyond that, where the ice maiden waited.

Using some twigs, Gabriel made a warm fire. Phineaus and Tilly had sent him off well supplied for the remainder of his journey, and he pulled a canteen filled with water and some crusty bread out of his satchel. He ate and drank heartily as he watched the night chase away the last remaining threads of sunset.

"How beautiful," he said to himself. "I wish I could share this with someone." And of all the people he'd met in his travels, it was the Gypsy who he wished was sitting beside him. He put away his canteen and pulled out a wool blanket, then slept a dreamless sleep.

Gabriel awoke to the early morning light against his eyelids. He packed up his supplies and started down the other side of the mountain toward the forest. The journey down was considerably easier than the ascent had been, and it didn't take Gabriel very long to arrive at the beginning of the forest.

He moved through the leafy trees while listening to the sound of chattering birds and the rustling of woodland animals. Branches and leaves crunched beneath his boots as he continued onward. Before too long the world became familiar again and he quickly found himself at the edge of the Frozen Forest. It seemed lifetimes since he'd last been here—but in truth, it had only been a few months. The area, which was so familiar to him, seemed changed somehow. "Maybe it's just that I've changed," Gabriel murmured.

He thought about how close the ice maiden was and part of him wished to forgo his appointment with the goblin and head straight to the cave. Would she be the same as he remembered? Or had he imagined her into something she was not?

Darkness was winding its way through the trees, Gabriel shivered as the air grew colder. He traveled to the very edge of the forest and searched for the rock formation the Gypsy told him to find. Gabriel discovered one that seemed the right size and shape, and pulled the carved feather from his pocket. Praying he would say the magic words right, he shouted, "*Thog…hairm Coi..meá…daí!*"

A loud rumbling filled the air and Gabriel gave an involuntary tremble. The winds picked up violently and a deep booming voice called out, "Whosoever seeks me out shall find only—". The words cut off mid-sentence and the winds swirled into a purple cyclone from which the Goblin emerged.

"Klaarg. Ye again? Ye certainly lookin' strange these days."

"Again?" questioned Gabriel. He stared at the Goblin and wondered how people could be afraid of something so small. The creature was odd to be sure, but there was nothing remotely fearsome about the Goblin. He was only as tall as Gabriel's knee and the most dangerous item he carried was a fishing lure hanging from a tarnished chain he wore across his neck. "The Gypsy sent me to see you. She said you owed her a favor and that you'd help me as repayment of that debt. She gave me a peacock feather as proof, but I lost it in a storm at sea. I do have a carved feather I made myself—if a feather is somehow important in this transaction." The Goblin's eyes narrowed and he looked Gabriel over slowly from head to toe.

"Klaarg, the Gypsy, ye say? She's the one done sent ye?"

"Yes, I'd never have found you otherwise."

A strange glimmer filled the Goblin's eyes. "Raag, ferget the feather—she only gave it ta ye fer proof. No need though, if she didna send ye, ye wouldn't know 'bout it a'tall. Now what do ye want?"

"I'm looking for a relic—a charm of some kind that's incredibly powerful. They say disaster follows wherever it goes."

The Goblin raised an eyebrow and asked, "Klaarg, and what'll ye be doin' with it if ye was ta find it? Ye just said yerself, ye don' know nothin' 'bout magic."

"I need to bring someone to life—I guess something. I'm a sculptor—I carve things and I carved a lady in ice, now I want to bring her to life."

"Raag, seems more easy to jus' find yerself a nice regular girl ta me. 'Specially fer a feller like ye. That's some big magic yer talkin' 'bout. Yer not the first one ta be tryin' this type a thin' and it ain't fer the weak. I can't be sure, but I think what yer lookin' fer is an ole medallion. Raag, an the last feller I saw that 'ad it ain't one who'll be lettin' it go easy."

"Where can I find him?"

The Goblin waved his hand in a circle and made a tight fist. When he opened it, a small silver compass lay shining against his green skin. "This here compass doesna point north—it shows ya where the strongest magic be. It should take ya ta that medallion—or at least ta whoever has it. Now ya can tell the Gypsy we're settled up."

"What did the Gypsy do for you anyway?"

"Raag, she found me somethin' that I lost."

"That's it?"

"Raag, some thin's are too 'portant to lose."

"Thank you for your help," Gabriel whispered as he stared at the compass and followed its quivering arrow.

"Raag. Thank ye," whispered the Goblin to himself. "This'll be ta best trick I ever played."

7

Remembering & Forgetting

An unearthly voice drifted through the green woods. *"Dearmad dhuine,"* it called faintly. *"Déan dearmad go léir."* The song was familiar to Sebastian.

That loathsome Witch, he thought, *always singing of forgetting. She'll wish she could forget the day she stole what's mine.* He trudged through the woods, angrily pushing aside branches that dared to get in his way. Sebastian had made up his mind--he would get his medallion back again and no one-- no matter how clever or powerful— would stop him.

Gabriel, on the other hand, had never heard a song like that before. There was nothing in his experience that compared to it. The Goblin's compass had led him to the swamp, and when he'd heard that strange tune, he'd been drawn to the source of the melody. Now, he drew closer and started to forget things.

First, he forgot the odd Goblin and the kindly fisherman and his wife, then the lost Brishen with his golden owl. Next, the memory of his beloved Gypsy slipped away. One by one all the things he'd seen and cared about had vanished from his thoughts. When he finally stood before the Swamp Witch, even the vision of the Ice Maiden's face had been erased from his mind. "*Dearmad,*" she sang as her bluish arms beckoned Gabriel toward her "*Dearmad dhuine.*"

Like a sleepwalker in a happy dream, Gabriel moved nearer to the Swamp Witch. "Closer," he whispered, "I must get closer." Suddenly Gabriel was close enough to stare directly into her piercing gray eyes. "*Déan dearmad go léir,*" she sang.

Some people call things that happen by chance a coincidence, others call them fate. Be it simple luck or a matter of destiny, it so happened that at the very moment our dear Gabriel was ensnared by the Swamp Witch, Sebastian arrived at the swamp.

Standing unnoticed several feet away behind Gabriel, Sebastian saw the other man moving helplessly toward the singing Witch. *She thinks she can steal from me! Well, I'll just steal from her!* Sebastian thought.

"*Stad!*" bellowed Sebastian and abruptly the Swamp Witch's song stopped. Gabriel too stopped motionless at the edge her lagoon. Sebastian moved nearer to them both and the Swamp Witch turned her head and sang an angry response to Sebastian's timely interruption.

> "*Foolish you must be*
> *To interrupt my melody*
> *You have disturbed my prey*
> *For which there is a price to pay!*"

"Your words have no power over me! You think you can trick *me*—you think you can *steal* from *me!* Now I shall steal from you!" And with that, Sebastian grabbed Gabriel by the shoulder, whirled him around and broke the trance.

A gasp emerged from Sebastian's throat and Gabriel's eyes widened in disbelief. "What magic is this!" shouted Sebastian.

Two pairs of identical blue eyes stared at each other. Two matching faces—exactly the same. Their bodies the same height, their hair the same deep black—every aspect of their person--down to their fingernails were as similar as two drops of rain. If not for their different clothing, you might have thought it was one man standing in front of a mirror. "Who are you! Why do you have my face!" Sebastian screamed again. "What magic is this!"

"Oh my god!" cried Johanna.

"Now this is some real magic!" called out Casper.

"You think it's some kind of crazy spell?" Johanna wondered aloud, as Mrs. Kinder stacked the empty bowls and dirty dishes in the sink.

"Maybe they've gone cuckoo and they just think they look the same," replied Casper as he took one finger and made a circle in the air near his ear.

Just then, the phone rang loud and shrill, causing the children to jump. Mrs. Kinder reached over and grabbed the receiver. "Hello, Emily." She answered.

Johanna gulped and leaned in to listen.

"Of course that makes sense. Don't worry about it, it's really no problem. I'm sure it will be easier for the children if they sleep in their own beds. I'm sure your guest room is more than sufficient. I'll just have Johanna unlock the doors— "

"Can I talk to my mother," Johanna interrupted.

"Me too!" Casper chimed in. "I want to talk too." Johanna glowered in response.

"That's all right, Emily dear, I know you have to go. I'll tell the children. We'll head over to the house lickety split, so if you need to reach us, call over there. Goodnight."

"You didn't let me talk!" Johanna exclaimed angrily.

"Me neither!" Casper added.

"Your mother was in a rush and couldn't talk for long. She needs to stay overnight at the hospital, so it looks like we're going to have a bit of a sleepover."

"Sleepover? *Here*?" Casper said, not trying to hide his dismay.

Mrs. Kinder laughed. "Of course not, we'll all go to your house and I'll sleep in the guest room. I'll take care of these dishes tomorrow." Mrs. Kinder wiped her hands on her apron, removed it and hung it on a peg. "I'm just going to run upstairs and gather a few things

I'll need for the night. You both grab your things and put your coats on."

The children started off down the hall.

"I can't believe she's sleeping in our house!" Casper exclaimed, as he began to put on his blue coat.

"We can't let anyone find out about this," Johanna replied.

"Of course not! We'd be tortured."

"I just don't want funny looks and whispers."

"We already get those," Casper answered, matter-of-factly. "I just don't want my head in a toilet."

"I'm tired of kids whispering when we walk in a room, or acting funny around us," Johanna answered as she tugged on her green wool pea coat.

"I'm tired of not being asked to do stuff anymore and being stuck with you all the time. I miss James and Benjie—playing pirates, isn't the same when you don't have anyone to walk the plank or swordfight with."

"Marcy stopped calling me too."

"Good. Marcy's *terrible*," said Casper.

"She's my best friend!"

"She *was* your best friend. We don't have friends anymore."

"That's not true. Mom says they're just confused—"

"Whatever. When Dad comes home everything will be like it used to be." Casper answered.

Unless he doesn't come home. Johanna thought. *Then things will never be the same.*

Mrs. Kinder chose that moment to emerge from the staircase, carrying an upholstered bag. It was an odd shape, sort of like an octagon and was printed with navy roses. It occurred to Johanna that she'd never seen a rose that color in real life.

"All right children, are you ready to go?"

"Yes!" Casper cried.

"But what about the story?" Johanna asked.

"We can continue it over at your house."

"But I didn't see you bring the book?" said Johanna.

"Oh of course, child. Thank you for reminding me. Sometimes I think I'd forget my head if it weren't attached." Mrs. Kinder went back for the golden book and joined Casper and Johanna in the hall. "Okay, it's time for us to be off."

Casper ran toward the door and out onto the porch.

"Casper! How many times has Mom told you not to run like that!" Johanna cried as she ran out after him. Mrs. Kinder chuckled to herself, locked the door behind her and followed the children across the street.

Johanna and Casper were both tucked into Johanna's bed after they'd each changed into their pajamas.

"Casper, stop squirming already!" said Johanna.

"I'm not squirming—I'm getting comfortable!" Casper replied.

"Why can't you just sleep in your own bed?"

"Of course, I'll sleep ALONE in my own bed when there's a WITCH in the house!"

Johanna sighed. "How many times have I told you that she's not a witch. She's just an old lady who likes weird old stuff."

"Yeah, right, whatever. But I'm sleeping with one eye open."

"That's not even possible, dimwit."

"It is, I heard it on some old TV show. And if it's not, I'll sleep with BOTH eyes open."

"It would serve you right if I kicked you out of this bed," said Johanna.

"Just try it, and I'll use my ninja skills on you— "

"Children," Mrs. Kinder said, interrupting Casper and startling both kids, as she walked into the room. "I think it's getting close to your bedtime, so if we want to sneak in a bit more of the story we're going to have to get started."

Mrs. Kinder pulled up the white wooden chair that was next to Johanna's desk and positioned it next to the bed and alongside the nightstand with the stained-glass lamp. Once again she held the book up so all Johanna could see was the gold leather cover. The book didn't have a title on it and Johanna wondered if the lettering had just rubbed away over time or if it there had never been a title in the first place. But what kind of book has no title on the cover?

"So where were we?" Mrs. Kinder asked as she adjusted her glasses.

"At the GOOD part." Casper said. "Gabriel and Sebastian finally meet and they look exactly alike."

"That is a good part." Mrs. Kinder replied. "That will take us right back to the swamp and the swamp witch."

"Now are you going to tell us why they look the same?" Johanna asked as she pulled up her comforter to cover herself.

"All in good time my dear," Mrs. Kinder answered. "All in good time."

"You—you're just like me," replied Gabriel in awe, resisting the urge to touch the other man's face and see if he was real. "How is this possible?"

Sebastian spun around to face the Swamp Witch. "What have you done! You will pay for this false magic!" Her voice took on a mocking tone and her lips curved up at the ends in a laughing smirk.

> *"Magic is not the root of this seed*
> *And I have no part in this deed.*
> *If it is answers that you desire*
> *Look toward your own sire."*

"Sire? *My* sire? My father? You mock me, Witch! I am not one of your pathetic prey. I'll make you suffer for your lies!"

An evil light sparkled in the Swamp Witch's stone-colored eyes and when her song began again her voice was even darker.

> *"The words I speak are only truth*
> *The answers lie within your youth*
> *Since you do not believe my song,*
> *I will show you that you're wrong."*

Right after the last word of the song pierced through the air, a thunderous sound filled the woods like the stampeding of a thousand wild horses.

Before Sebastian could utter a single magic word, or Gabriel begin to even contemplate this turn of events, a dark green smoke emerged from the swamp and flood-ed through the trees. It was thick and cold and smelled like fish left out in the sun to rot. It covered everything until they could see nothing g but smoke.

The pair coughed, forcefully trying to empty their lungs of the foul air. As the smoke cleared, they found they were no longer in the swamp.

Their new location was a warm, sunny village lined with iron lampposts and wood barrels full of purple and orange flowers. Just down a short blue cobblestone path there was a market with children playing and villagers selling their wares.

Gabriel gazed around at his surroundings, amazed at what had happened and wondering why the town looked familiar to him.

Meanwhile, Sebastian squinted and stared pointedly at Gabriel's shabby fisherman's garb; carefully looking over each detail of the stranger's face, searching for even the tiniest difference that might give the man's identity away. *If anyone who knows me had seen this man, they would have thought he was me. If he'd come across any of my enemies, he'd never have survived. He's either more resourceful than he appears, or incredibly lucky. Still, it's going to be problematic to have him running around. Once I figure out who or what he is, I'll have to take care of him.*

"What are you?" demanded Sebastian darkly.

Gabriel was startled by Sebastian's harsh tone. He considered the man's torn and bloody clothes, thinking *He wasn't afraid of the Swamp Witch—not in the slightest and still he seems far more concerned with who I am than where we are. No matter how much he looks like me, he's dangerous and I must take care.*

"I'm just an artist—a sculptor actually."

"Hmm," replied Sebastian, "that's odd since you're wearing fisherman's clothes."

"I am?" questioned Gabriel.

"Don't you know the difference or are you just playing at being an idiot?" Sebastian replied, raising his voice.

Gabriel looked down at the clothes he was wearing. "I-I don't understand. These aren't my clothes—I don't know where they came from. I've never seen them before—this isn't what I started wearing today."

"Are you actually trying to make me believe the Swamp Witch changed your clothes? If so, you truly are an imbecile."

"No, no—of course not."

"So, why are you at the swamp and what mysteriously changed your clothes?

"I don't know," replied Gabriel as he searched his memory for answers to Sebastian's question. A bubble of panic grew inside him as he realized that he couldn't remember. "I can't remember. The last thing I remember is looking for firewood near my home."

"You probably lost your way in the trees, then stumbled into the swamp."

"Makes sense," replied Gabriel a bit hesitantly. "That doesn't explain why I find it so hard to remember certain things, the most recent things in fact. I remember things from when I was a child, but there seems to be something missing."

"Her song must have affected you. She uses it to lure in unsuspecting victims. She makes them forget everything in their life—the longer they listen, the more they forget, until they can't remember anything at all. It's only a spell that makes her voice enticing; otherwise it sounds like someone choking the life out of a buzzard."

Gabriel was wise enough not to ask how the man knew what sound a buzzard made when you strangled it, and instead asked "If that's the case then why aren't you affected?"

"Her magic only effects *regular* people," replied Sebastian with an arrogant tilt of his head.

"You're magical too then?" asked Gabriel. "That's why you're immune?"

"Took quite a bit of time to piece that together."

"Magic isn't my specialty."

"Well, then you'll have to learn fast, because there's no escaping it."

"So why were you visiting the Swamp Witch?"

"She took something that belongs to me," replied Sebastian.

"Wouldn't it be easier and safer to just find another elsewhere?"

"No one takes what's mine," Sebastian answered coldly, his voice as sharp as a blade.

"Well stealing is never---"

"As I said," interrupted Sebastian harshly. "No one takes what's mine—take care to remember that."

"So if you're immune to her magic, how did we end up here? She must have cast some kind of spell?"

"Are you calling me a liar?" responded Sebastian hotly.

"No, I'm just trying to understand how this works and where we are," answered Gabriel, frustration lining his voice.

"That stupid witch cast a spell on both of us. I'm immune to her song because I long ago cast a spell to protect myself from it, but this spell is different."

"Well if you're so handy with spells can't you cast one to get us out of here?"

"I was going to get to that as soon as I figured out who you are, which would be a far easier task if your memory wasn't as full of holes as a giant's sock."

"Not all of us are magicians." answered Gabriel.

Sebastian gave out an unexpected laugh. "What an absurd idea. For a forgetful artist wearing fisherman's clothes you are quite entertaining. But it's time to end the nonsense and get out of here."

Sebastian took a moment to concentrate and in a firm voice said, *"Seal sos."* Nothing happened and the two men remained in the village. Again, Sebastian repeated, *"Seal sos."* There wasn't so much as the faintest breeze in response.

"Are you sure those are the right words?" asked Gabriel.

"Of course, you moron!" bellowed Sebastian. "They mean break the spell and that's what we're trying to do. Magic isn't always precise—not that I'd expect someone like *you* to understand that. I swear I will make that Swamp Witch pay for turning us into living bookends and saddling me with some sort of imbecilic version of myself!"

What Gabriel lacked in magical understanding he made up for in powers of observation. Now was his opportunity to take better control of the situation, but first he'd have to calm and distract Sebastian. "Perhaps we should figure out where we are—maybe that's the problem with your spell and once we know that, your magical words will work."

"Since you've found a sudden intellect, what do you suggest we do first?" asked Sebastian.

LISA PREZIOSI

"Why don't we just ask someone, there seem to be plenty of people around. I'm sure they can tell us what town we're in," replied Gabriel, matter of factly.

"Don't you find it odd that none of them have paid us even the slightest bit of attention?"

"They're probably just minding their business."

"Yes, of course, that's exactly what villagers love to do when they see strangers—particularly two oddly-dressed strangers that happen to look exactly alike and just magically appeared in their village square." Sebastian laughed. "Yes, of course, they'd mind their own business."

"I don't understand."

"That's apparently a common theme for you, so why don't you go ask someone here to enlighten you? Perhaps that will clarify things."

Gabriel walked down the blue cobblestone path toward the village square and toward a young woman in a pink dress selling apples out of a small covered wagon. He stood directly in front of her cart, but she paid him no heed. "Excuse me, miss." The woman did not so much as blink an eye. "Please miss, my friend and I are lost, can you tell me where we are?" Still she did not acknowledge Gabriel. "If I buy one of your lovely apples will you answer my question?" Gabriel leaned down to grab one of the shiny red apples, but his hand went right through it as though it were smoke.

"Things any clearer to you now?" called Sebastian, who had quietly walked up behind him. Gabriel turned to face him and saw Sebastian leaning against an iron lamppost with his arms folded across his chest, a mocking grin on his face. Gabriel walked toward him.

"Does this mean we're dead?"

"It's doubtful the afterlife would be in a simple village where only we can see each other. It's even more doubtful that that vindictive witch would be able to finish me. I'm far too powerful for that."

The frustration that had been steadily building in Gabriel since he'd met the mysterious and horribly overbearing stranger finally burst out. "Of course, so powerful that you can't get us out of here even though you're the one who made the Swamp Witch angry enough to send us here in the first place!"

"Interesting commentary from someone who would have been a rotting corpse had I not intervened," replied Sebastian haughtily.

"At this point, I'd probably be better off that way," replied Gabriel, his voice tightening.

"If you'd like me to arrange that I'd be happy to do so, just say the word."

Gabriel let out a deep sigh. "We need to stop this bickering—it's pointless. And you're right I wouldn't have survived without your help and for that I'm quite grateful, so let's focus on what's important. What do you think is going on here? Are we ghosts?"

"In a manner of speaking. If I had to guess, I'd say that the witch cast another kind of memory charm and she's sent us into the past," replied Sebastian.

"The past?"

"I'm guessing she sent us back in time. We can't touch anything or change anything, just watch. I've never performed this kind of spell before since it's pretty useless, but what else would you expect from a Swamp Witch."

"Who's past are we in? Yours, or mine?" asked the Gabriel.

"I've never seen this place before so it must be yours."

"It does seem a little familiar," Gabriel said uncertainly.

"It's probably from some of the memories you're missing. Lucky for you that spell wears off once you're away from the witch. You should start slowly remembering things."

Gabriel looked around the village. "Nothing is specifically coming back to me, but it does remind me of the village where I grew up. But it's never warm and sunny there—it's snowy and frozen."

"That certainly doesn't sound like this place," grumbled Sebastian.

"Unless of course it wasn't always frozen," answered Gabriel thoughtfully. "I have an idea."

"This should be good."

"You'll have to trust me."

Sebastian let out a huge laugh. "You're showing your idiocy again—trusting anyone is a fool's mistake."

"What choice do you have?"

"I could cast a spell to turn you into a bug, so you'd fly off and leave me in peace." *Or so I could squash you flat*, thought Sebastian.

So you could squash me, thought Gabriel silently. "Then you'd never know where you are and be trapped here."

He's not as stupid as I thought, Sebastian mused. "Possibly, or maybe getting rid of you would send me back, since this is most likely your past."

"But you're the one the witch specifically sent here. For all you know I'm just your guide."

"What exactly did you have in mind?" asked Sebastian suspiciously.

"I'm going to act as though this is the same village—the one I grew up near and head toward my home. That will at least tell us if we're in that place or not. It's only a few miles west. What do you say?"

"As you mentioned, I have no choice." *At least for now*, thought Sebastian.

"Then we're agreed. We'll head west and hope that we find some answers," said Gabriel, forcing his voice to sound hopeful.

The two walked through the square, one carrying a leather satchel, the other wearing a dark, torn cloak. They left the village together, their anxious steps moving in perfect symmetry.

"Anything familiar?" asked Sebastian.

"Vaguely," replied Gabriel.

The men walked further from town, passing open fields of sunflowers, their yellow petals bloomed cheerfully against the bright sky. "It looks similar to my home, but I don't ever remember seeing flowers there," Gabriel continued.

Down a grassy slope with scattered rocks, Gabriel's cabin came into view, or at least it resembled his cabin. The structure had a bright coat of white paint with the greenest ivy twining around it. Blue shutters adorned the windows and were open as if to say "welcome." All around the cottage were small bushes filled with tiny purple flowers that captured the attention of countless butterflies.

"It can't be," Gabriel murmured. "It's never looked like this before, except in my dreams," his voice trailing off into a whisper.

At Gabriel's mention of the word dream, Sebastian shivered. A small flicker of a memory formed at the edge of his mind. The flowers, the butterflies, they were familiar; he too had seen them in his dreams. And this place, there was something about it that felt like a memory. *Hogwash!* he thought. *It's just that witch's spell. This place means nothing to me.*

At that moment, the soft humming of a melody filled the air, making both Sebastian and Gabriel turn their heads. "I know that voice. I've heard it before," said Gabriel as he quickly moved to the side of the house to find the source.

Sebastian hurriedly followed behind him, never mentioning that the voice was achingly familiar to him as well.

At the back of the cottage, a woman with long hair as dark and shiny as onyx was hanging wet clothing up on a clothesline and humming a song to herself. Gabriel and Sebastian walked nearer, paying no attention to each other.

"Mama!" two tiny voices cried in perfect unison.

"Mother," the Gabriel and Sebastian whispered at the same time, turning to see two small boys about four years old run out to the yard with tears falling down their red faces. They looked identical with black hair that curled around their temples and startling blue eyes.

"Gabriel hit me," said the little one on the left.

"Only cause 'Bastian hit me first," answered Gabriel sticking his tongue out at his brother.

"He deserved it Mama, he called me a troll!"

Their mother let out a laugh and grabbed the two of them in her arms, pulling them into a warm hug. The boys cuddled into her embrace. "Whatever am I going to do with you two?" She punctuated the question with a noisy kiss on each their heads. "Always fighting…but if I try to separate you, you'll cry even more."

"Gabriel's the cry baby. I'd be just fine," answered the tiny Sebastian.

"So you'd be perfectly happy if we sent Gabriel away?" their mother asked.

"I'd be *very* happy," Sebastian replied, nodding his head.

"No Mama, don't send me away!" cried Gabriel as he clung to her tightly.

"My darling, I'd never send you away, either of you. You're the sun and the moon to me." She pulled them back, so she could look into their matching eyes. "Always remember that no matter how much you fight, or how much you think you'd be happier on your own, you are brothers and you need each other."

"I don't need him," answered Gabriel crossly. "He's mean."

"And I don't need him, he's just a big baby!" exclaimed Sebastian.

"No matter who's mean or a baby, or silly or scared, you're brothers and nothing in the whole wide world will ever change that." She smoothed out the hair on each of their heads and pushed them toward the cottage door. "Now how about you gather up your blocks and play here while I hang up the laundry. Your father will be home soon."

"Okay, Mama," replied Sebastian and ran inside to gather up the blocks.

Gabriel didn't move and instead stood solemn eyed watching his Mother. "You wouldn't really send me away, would you?"

She pulled him close to her and looked deep into his eyes. "Never, baby. My heart would break right in half. I love you and your brother and your father so very much." She gave him another kiss. "Now go help your brother before he takes all the blocks for himself."

With that Gabriel rushed out of her arms and into the house, yelling out, "Bastian those blocks are mine too!"

A worried expression crossed their mother's face, one the little boys hadn't seen, but that the older Sebastian and Gabriel noticed. She waited until the twins came back outside with their blocks and once they were settled, she turned back to the laundry.

"'Bastian?" asked the older Gabriel as he stared at the grown-up Sebastian.

"Nobody calls me that," Sebastian answered.

"I did."

"I don't remember," Sebastian replied trying to make his voice sound firm as he turned away from Gabriel.

"You do, you just saw. You remember her, don't you? I remember more now, I remember you. I'd forgotten. It was like a dream before, little bits and pieces of memories I couldn't put together."

"I don't know what you're talking about. I didn't have parents! That's not me-that's not—"

Gabriel grabbed Sebastian by the shoulders. "You saw it. You know. You remember. Don't lie to me!" Sebastian pushed Gabriel to the ground.

"It can't be real! Don't you understand! If it's real, she abandoned us!" Sebastian exclaimed in a fury. "She separated us!" Angry tears threatened to fall from his eyes, but he used all his willpower to stop them. "If that's our mother, then she didn't care enough about us to take care of us, or keep us together, or safe. She left us!"

Gabriel struggled to his feet. "Not by choice! She's dead." With those simple words, the longing and hope of an entire lifetime died.

Gabriel's voice softened as he realized the impact of what he was telling Sebastian. *He doesn't know, he's been wondering all this time. He's losing them all over again.* "Father too. I don't know how, or why. Growing up I'd visit their graves."

"She's gone? They're gone?" Sebastian paused and felt the crack in his heart open up and grief spill out. He watched the beautiful woman hang clothes on the line and walked up to her. "She didn't leave me on purpose? She didn't leave me alone with her?"

Her? Gabriel wondered. *Who? What happened to him?* Gabriel knew it wasn't the time to ask and instead walked up behind Sebastian. "I don't think she would do that, to either of us."

"Something was wrong. Something happened to them. There was fear in her face a moment ago."

"You saw it, too," said Gabriel.

"Margarite!" a man's voice called out. "Margarite," the voice called out more anxiously, as a cart and horse pulled up. A tall man with sandy-colored hair and piercing blue eyes jumped off the horse and ran toward the house.

"Papa!" the boys called out in unison and turned toward him. Their father quickly changed the expression on his face and gave them a smile.

"Papa, guess what, Gabriel hit me!"

"'Bastian hit me first!"

"Peanuts, I can't keep up with your fighting. Now gather up your blocks and bring them inside, we're all going on a little trip."

"A trip?" the boys asked, once again in unison.

"Yes, it's going to be an adventure, now hurry up, while I talk to your mother." The children ran inside and he turned to face their mother. "She found us."

With those words, Margarite's face paled. She dropped the wet shirt she'd been holding. "No."

Their father placed a hand on her shoulder and pulled her into his arms. "T'will be all right, love. The cart is ready, just grab what we need."

"The boys are so little, we have to keep them safe."

"There's too much to do now to be afraid. Just hurry."

Margarite ran into the house with her husband following close behind. "Boys, we have to go." she called out to them as she entered.

"You see!" bellowed Sebastian, turning to face Gabriel. "Someone is after them, and that someone is going to be what kills them! We have to do something!"

Quickly, the family emerged from the cabin, each parent holding one of the boys, and rushed to the horse and cart. Margarite settled them onto the bags her husband threw in the cart, while he readied the horses.

"Sebastian," the older Gabriel said as he placed his hand on his brother's arm to calm him. "We can't do anything. This is already done—finished. They can't even see us— "

"There has to be something—We have to go with them."

"How can we? We can't go in their cart and we're not fast enough to keep up with it."

"We have to follow them—we have to!" Sebastian bellowed. "Stop," he called out to his father. But his father could not hear him and instead hopped into the driver's seat.

"Ready, Margarite?" he called out.

"No!" cried Sebastian.

"Yes, hurry," she replied.

"No!" cried Sebastian again, but they did not listen to him and the carriage drove off down the dirt road and away from the cabin. Sebastian watched as his parents moved farther away from him. His face grew hard and still.

"Bastian— "

"I told you not to call me that." Sebastian answered coldly.

"This is already done—there's nothing we can do to change things—"

"I know that. You're the idiot who didn't even know this was the past." Sebastian's anger seemed to bubble up like a stew that's been simmering in a pot much longer than it should have. "The show is over now, so why are we still here. What's next!" he screamed, his voice taking on a terrifying tone as he looked toward the sky. "You stupid witch! Is that the best you can do? Is this all you have for me!"

An eerie laugh rang through the air. It grew so loud that it made the ground rumble and shake violently, knocking both men off their feet. A large crack split the earth, sending Sebastian tumbling downward.

"No!" shouted Gabriel as he reached for Sebastian, but it was too late and Sebastian plummeted down into the growing chasm. A pain stabbed through Gabriel like a pickaxe into ice. "I won't lose you again!" he shouted. And without thinking of the consequences (or much of anything, besides saving Sebastian), Gabriel jumped into the darkness after him and fell and fell.

8

LOST & FOUND

Sebastian felt lightness in his head and stomach as he somersaulted into the darkness. Deeper and deeper he fell, until the light from the above world was as small as the tip of pin. Before he could even begin to worry about his unfortunate predicament, he landed on his shoulder with a hard thud. The ground felt firm and the air smelled of dampness and moss. From above, he heard a flapping noise.

With a crash Gabriel came tumbling down, falling on top of Sebastian.

"Can't you do anything right?!" bellowed Sebastian as he pushed Gabriel off. It was too dark to make out anything but Gabriel's silhouette. "You're like a toddler, always causing problems."

"Me? I'm the one causing problems?" Gabriel asked as the fear he'd felt at almost losing his brother evaporated. "You're the hothead who keeps challenging the witch who's holding us captive. Brother or not, sorcerer or not, you're going to stop this nonsense, or we'll never get out of here and I *have* to get out of here."

"Some urgent appointment?" asked Sebastian mockingly.

"I-I don't remember exactly. I just know that there's something important I'm supposed to do."

"Ah yes dear brother, this is the perfect time for you to be pondering the meaning of your existence."

"No," replied Gabriel firmly as he struggled to stand. "Not my life, but a specific task—there's something I was supposed to do—or find, before the Swamp Witch interrupted me."

Sebastian let out a sigh, but silently felt a prickle of suspicion rise up inside him. "Again with the useless whining about your memory—I told you, you'll get it back slowly."

"Fine," answered Gabriel, anger making his voice sharp. "So what do we do now, oh powerful and perfect one?"

As if in response to Gabriel's question, a blinding light filled the darkness. "What now!" exclaimed Gabriel, in frustration. The light dimmed to reveal that the two men were standing in a cave. Up ahead of them was a tunnel and farther along, there appeared to be a torch light glowing.

"Come on," urged Sebastian, motioning for Gabriel to follow. "And try not to get yourself killed, or maimed."

"So many people in the world and I get the most arrogant and egotistical one as my twin brother," muttered Gabriel under his breath, as he followed behind Sebastian.

Sebastian walked ahead carefully through the stone corridor. *It can't be,* he thought. *This is the ice maiden's cave. What does this mean?*

All the while, Gabriel couldn't shake the feeling that he had been to this cave before and that there was something very urgent he was supposed to do. There was a deep ache in his heart that had no name or face attached. *I know this place and it's important—it's part of what I'm supposed to do. Sebastian said I will remember. I just hope it's not too late when I do.*

They rounded a corner and came to an open area. They came upon their four-year-old selves sleeping on a blanket in the corner. There were bags of food and a small fire burning. An older man and woman stood away from the children speaking in hushed tones. "Grandfather!" exclaimed the older Gabriel. "He looks younger—but it's him—and that must be Grandmother. He's talking! He never talked—not in all the years I knew him."

That's not the grandmother I grew up with, Sebastian thought. He eyed the worried faces of his grandparents and said, "Come on! We have to hear what they're saying." They hurried closer.

"She'll be coming for them soon. There's only so long Margarite and Gregory can lead her on a wild goose chase. We must come up with a plan, Silas," said their grandmother.

"She's strong," Silas answered. His voice deep and sad—it sounded just the way that Gabriel had always thought it would. "I don't know where she's gotten so much power from. But we can't run. And I don't know how long we can hide."

"You're right. But we can't let her have them."

Silas paused, a pained expression on his face. "She doesn't want both of them. She only wants one. The amulet's prophecy didn't mention there were two boys—just that there was a child. He paused again, and a somber light filled his eyes. We can hide one of them—save one of them."

Horror filled their grandmother's face. "And what, sacrifice the other?"

"No, we can try to save him too. But if we hide one—use a little magic to cover the trail, she'll never know he exists. He'll be perfectly safe. You can stay with him—hide for a while and in a few years, go to a little village and build him a good life. I'll take the other and do my best to keep him safe."

"And how do we choose? How do we choose which one to save and which one to put in that monster's path?" Tears fell from their grandmother's face. "Look at them!" She pointed to the boys sleeping with their arms around each other. "How can we separate them!"

"I don't want to do this either. But what choice do we have?"

"What will Margarite and Gregory say? They would never want us to do this!"

"Gregory and Margarite are probably dead—and if they're not, they will be soon." Silas replied.

"No," she cried. "Our beautiful daughter—her wonderful husband. And those two little babies. Why is there so much evil in this world?"

Silas pulled her to him and held her in his arms, stroking her hair softly and brushing her tears away. In a hushed voice, he continued. "There's evil, but there's goodness too. We can save one and do our best to save the other. If we keep the boys together, she'll take them both—and do god knows what with the one she decides is useless to her."

"You're right, of course. Which one does she want—Gabriel or Sebastian?"

"I'm not sure. Sebastian is first born, so he's my best guess. You take Sebastian. I'll keep Gabriel with me," replied Silas grimly.

"So it's little Gabriel who'll be in danger?"

"I'm afraid so—I think it's Sebastian she wants for her spells, so if we keep him away from her—not only will it keep Sebastian safe, but it will keep her from becoming even more powerful."

The grown-up Sebastian listened intently. This woman he saw before him—with the kind eyes and the blue dress--this wasn't the grandmother he'd known. The woman he'd known was cruel and merciless—and a murderer. And he'd wager a mountain of gold that the "she" they were referring to was Malvina.

"You have enough supplies to last at least a month. Stay here as long as possible. Then head out west to the fishing village on the Ambrian coast. It's quiet there and you'll be safe. If anyone asks, your family was killed in a terrible fire and you and your grandson are the only survivors. I'll cast a protection spell on the cave and take Gabriel now."

Silas pulled his wife close and gave her a gentle kiss. He walked over to the sleeping boys and gently pulled Gabriel out from Sebastian's arm. The little boy moaned in his sleep and then settled in the crook of his grandfather's neck. Little Sebastian turned over and then settled in once again.

Silas gave his wife a long, deep look. "Goodbye, my love. And if the gods should smile upon us—we'll all be together again." With that, Silas took a leather bag of supplies, whispered a soft incantation, and left the cave. Their grandmother sat down next to the sleeping Sebastian and stroked his hair.

Gabriel turned to Sebastian. "So, you were raised by our grandmother, while I was with grandfather."

"No," he answered, with a sharp edge to his voice.

"What do you mean—you told me your grandmother raised you?"

"She told me she was my grandmother. But that woman you see sitting there—that's not the woman who raised me. I think the woman they're talking about—the one who killed our parents, is the woman who raised me."

"What!" exclaimed Gabriel. "And what about the amulet and the prophecy?"

"I don't know," Sebastian lied.

Amulet, Gabriel thought. *That sounds familiar. I think that's what I'm looking for. Someone sent me— someone strange sent me to find it. I can't remember who. I can't tell Sebastian. He'll trust me even less then he does now.*

A frosty gust of wind blew through the cave, making ice crystals form on the cave walls. Their grandmother pulled the sleeping Sebastian into her arms, waking him up. "What happened gran'ma."

"She's right on time," said the older Sebastian. *I won't remember*, he thought. *I won't remember. I won't remember.*

Gabriel looked over at Sebastian and then saw the dark hooded figure approach the boy and his grandmother. "Leave us alone!" Their grandmother cried out. "We've done nothing to you. Just leave us be."

The figure let out a high-pitched cackle--the sound full of evil and wickedness. It made Gabriel shiver and Sebastian's spine stiffen like a fire poker. The little boy began to cry, "Gran'ma what's happening. Make it stop."

"It's okay Sebastian, just close your eyes."

"Yes, of course", said the hooded figure. "Close your eyes, dear boy. That way you won't watch your precious 'Gran-ma' die. "Thoghairm bás," the cloaked figure said coldly.

Grandmother's face turned suddenly pale and white. Her skin grew stiff like stone and her hands fell away from Sebastian. "Gran'ma," he cried. "Gran'ma!" Her eyes were unblinking and unmoving.

The figure moved closer to the little boy. "You belong to me now. And I suggest you stop crying, or else you're going to make me very, very mad. And you wouldn't want to do that, would you?" The little boy trembled with fear and his sobs turned to quiet streams of tears. The robed figure scooped him into her arms.

The grown Sebastian walked closer to the two figures as a horrified Gabriel could do nothing but watch in stunned silence. "You evil, vindictive hag. You're lucky I didn't remember this when I killed you. I'd have made your death last so much longer."

"You killed her?" asked Gabriel, still in shock over what he'd witnessed.

"Yes, dear brother. And I didn't make her suffer nearly as much as I should have."

"How? Why?"

"You just watched her murder your grandmother and presumably both of your parents. Isn't that reason enough?"

"Yes, but you didn't remember that before. And she's so powerful—you'd have to be more powerful than she was."

"I was more determined. You'd be surprised to what lengths true hatred can push you."

"What did she do to you?" Gabriel asked with concern as he gazed at what was left of his Grandmother.

"It wasn't about me." *Elise*, Sebastian thought, *sweet Elise. I made her pay for it. I made her pay for what she did to you.*

"I'm so sorry," replied Gabriel. "It must have been a terrible thing to have to do, but I understand why you killed her."

Sebastian let out a laugh and ignored the pain that pounded at his insides. "Awful? It was one of the best feelings I've ever had. If I'd remembered this then, it would have been even better."

After taking in Sebastian's dark words, Gabriel responded carefully, "She was a monster. Don't let her turn you into one as well."

"It's too late for that." Sebastian answered grimly. "It's done—all of this is done." After the last word had tumbled from Sebastian's lips, a deep gray fog rose from the cold stone floor and quickly enveloped the pair, making it impossible for them to see each other. "Looks like that stupid Swamp Witch isn't finished yet."

"Well, we saw what happened to you. I guess it's time to see what happened to me." A cool breeze began to blow and started to clear the fog a bit. Through the grayness emerged an iron lamppost which held a swinging lantern. It cast an eerie golden glow through the mist. Large snowflakes began to fall and the mist cleared enough to reveal that just beyond the lamppost was an iron fence with a wide gate.

"I know this place." said Gabriel. "It's the cemetery at the edge of town—right next to the old church where our parents are buried. Grandfather and I would visit all the time." Gabriel moved ahead to lead the way and follow a stone path through the gate. "I know the way to their graves. Follow me."

Sebastian didn't argue and instead simply followed. Ice and snow had begun to cover the surrounding trees making their leaves droop and fall. Through rows of old stones and up a small hill, they came to see Silas standing with bowed head, his large hand holding tight to young Gabriel's. All around them snowflakes fell.

"Is 'Bastian dead too?" asked little Gabriel, his head turned to look up at his solemn Grandfather.

"No, but he had to go away."

"I want to go too," said Gabriel.

"I know, but you can't. You must stay with me now. One day you'll see Sebastian again--"

"When! I want to see him now! I want Mommy and Daddy and Gran'ma too. Why can't I be dead too?" Gabriel sobbed. Silas picked the weeping child up into his arms.

"I'm sorry for all you've lost. And I know I'm not much, but you have me. And I promise one day you'll see Sebastian again, but probably not for a long time. I know that's hard, but things will get better." Silas took a deep breath and whispered to the sobbing child, *"Déan dearmad faoi Sebastian."*

An older Gabriel looked over at Sebastian, questioningly and Sebastian replied, "It's similar to the Swamp Witch's spell. He's making you forget me."

"Why!" replied Gabriel angrily. "It would have been better if I'd known, I would have come looking for you."

"And you'd have run into that lovely woman you just saw in cave." Sebastian shook his head. "He was trying to protect you—forgetting me was the best thing for you."

"And what about the best thing for you?" asked Gabriel.

Before Sebastian could reply Silas shut his eyes and spoke his last incantation. "*Tugaim mo ghlór, a cheilt ar an leanbh.*"

Then, carrying the softly sobbing child, he made his way out of the cemetery. "You know what that means, don't you," Gabriel asked, eyeing his brother suspiciously.

"Yes, yes I do. And I'll even translate it for you if you just say pretty pretty please," answered Sebastian.

"How about you tell it to me now, or I punch you until you do?"

Sebastian laughed, "That's something I'd love to see— "

"Don't tempt me."

"Yes, you have me shaking, really, Gabriel, I'm terrified."

"Sebastian," replied Gabriel menacingly.

"Fine, fine. But don't say I didn't try to teach you manners. Roughly translated his spell says "I give my voice, to hide this child."

"What?"

"Gabriel, you really need to work on your comprehension. He traded his voice and his ability to do magic to keep you safe."

"I don't understand," replied Gabriel.

"Hmm, let me break this down simply. Magic is like trading."

"Trading?"

"Yes. Spells like anything else have a price. Like an object. If you want a ruby necklace it will cost you a lot of gold. The cost of a spell isn't in gold, it's in sacrifice. The more you give up for the magic, the more powerful the spell will be. Our grandfather gave up his voice and his ability to do magic to keep you safe. Some people give up years of their lives—or even their souls to make a powerful spell."

What did you give up, wondered Gabriel. "So, that explains why he never spoke."

"What happened to him?" Sebastian asked suddenly.

"He died in his sleep, a little over a year ago."

"It was peaceful?"

Gabriel looked Sebastian over to see if any emotion flickered in his brother's face. "Certainly seemed so. I buried him next to our Grandmother and our parents. He'd be so happy to know you're alive."

"I'm not so sure about that." The falling snow became thicker and heavier. It piled up around the two men and in a matter of seconds it was up to their necks.

"Can't you do something?" asked Gabriel struggling to free himself from the snow. "With your magic?"

Sebastian instead stood still and immobile. "I tried before, it doesn't work here. And none of this is real anyway—you don't feel cold, do you?" Before Gabriel could answer Sebastian's question, the last of the snow covered them both and all they saw was white.

"I don't like this story anymore," replied Casper angrily. "I want to stop now."

"Don't worry, Casper. I'm sure it will turn out all right." Johanna answered. "Won't it, Mrs. Kinder?"

"I've always said that one can't decide full well if they like something or not until they've given it a proper chance. We've come this far, so let's just hold tight 'til the end—and maybe, just maybe you might like it after all," replied Mrs. Kinder.

"I don't want to hear any more!" he replied, unconvinced.

"But don't you want to see what happens to Gabriel and Sebastian when they face the Swamp Witch? And who ends up with the medallion? And if Gabriel finds the Gypsy? And if the ice maiden ever comes to life?" asked Johanna.

"Yes, but I'm tired of people dying. It's getting too sad." Casper answered.

"Does it get sadder?" Johanna asked Mrs. Kinder.

"Yes, and happier too, but it all depends on who we're watching at the time," Mrs. Kinder. "But I promise you it will all be worth it. Now let's get back to the story before it gets away from us."

As the two men stared into pure blankness, faint colors began to bleed through—subtle browns and greens emerged, like spilled paint seeping through an old cloth. In moments, they were back in the colorful swamp and facing the laughing Swamp Witch. She held out the golden medallion.

> *"To win this gift there is a way*
> *Your brother you must betray."*

Her eyes looked piercingly at Sebastian and then Gabriel. She lifted the medallion over her head and let it settle against her chest.

My medallion, thought Sebastian.

That's what I've been looking for. The thing the Goblin sent me for, thought Gabriel.

> *The cost to win this prize is high*
> *One of you will have to die.*
> *So fight each other to the death*
> *And when one takes his final breath,*
> *The survivor wins this amulet.*

The witch finished her song with a loud cackle. Gabriel turned to Sebastian and asked "What do we do now? We can't kill--" but before he could finish Sebastian pounced on top of him and they began rolling on the ground struggling. "You can't mean to do this 'Bastian—I'm your brother."

"I need that medallion!" With those words, Sebastian pulled the chisel from his cloak pocket and raised it over Gabriel.

That's my chisel, thought Gabriel frantically. *And my brother's going to kill me with it.* Sebastian aimed it over Gabriel's heart as Gabriel grabbed his wrist to hold the chisel back. All the while the Swamp Witch's horrid laugh filled the air.

Just as Sebastian managed to fight off Gabriel's defenses and bring the chisel right above his brother's heart, he shouted out, "*Muince malairte!*"

In a flash, the chisel in Sebastian's hand was replaced with the medallion and where the medallion had once hung on the witch's seaweed chest, the chisel was now plunged. The Swamp Witch let out a piercing scream while greenish black sludge poured from her wound. She pulled the chisel from her chest, throwing it across the swamp. It landed in the mud with a soft thud. The swamp around her bubbled as though a fire was making it boil over, and slowly, she sank into the mire. "*Dioltas!*" she cried out as she was sinking. "*Dioltas!*"

Gabriel looked away from this horrible scene and stared transfixed at the medallion hanging from his brother's hand. Gabriel reached his fingers out to touch it and brushed against the cold metal. Sebastian yanked it away and rolled off his brother. Gabriel picked up the chisel that had landed on the ground and struggled to stand.

"You killed her," said Gabriel with horror in his voice.

"She had my medallion."

"You killed her with my chisel."

"Yours?" answered Sebastian, in confusion.

"It's mine. I used it to carve the angel in the ice. I used it to create and you destroyed with it." Gabriel muttered dazedly, more to himself than Sebastian.

At this statement, Sebastian's eyes narrowed. *He carved the ice maiden. That's why he's been after this medallion too. He wants her for himself.*

"It was so fast—you killed her so easily." Gabriel shook his head, as though trying to shake the image from his mind. He continued his voice stronger, "But you didn't kill me."

"No, but I should have. You want this," Sebastian said motioning toward the medallion locked tightly in his fist. "This is mine. If you try to take it from me, I won't be so generous next time."

"Bastian, we can help each other- "

"No Gabriel. I have unfinished business to attend to and I can't have you following me. *Thoghairm codla-ta.*"

Gabriel felt an overwhelming tiredness come over him, while his brother's magic words rang in his ears.

*Thoghairm codlata —summon...sleep. Sebastian is put-
ting me to sleep.* Gabriel fell to his knees, his hand still
curved around his chisel. Gabriel's new understanding
of magic did not bring him any ability to fight the
spell.

"Goodbye Gabriel", said Sebastian, and then more
softly, "I wish things could be different."

Gabriel's body hit the damp earth of the swamp
with surprising gentleness and the last thing Gabriel
thought of was the Swamp Witch's final word—
Dioltas—Revenge.

9

BEGINNINGS & ENDINGS

Sebastian moved quickly through the woods, fighting the tiredness that seeped into the edges of his body. He had to get to the cave before Gabriel awoke. Gabriel was the other person the shadow in the mirrored castle had talked about, the other person who the medallion was gravitating toward. Sebastian couldn't afford to lose now, not when he was so close to success.

The memories of everything he'd witnessed during his trip to the past drifted through his mind. The sadness clung to him like wet clothes after you're caught in a sudden rainstorm.

Why did those memories matter? Why did it matter that his parents hadn't abandoned him? That his family had wanted him? That his real grandmother had died protecting him? It was too late to change any of it, too late to care about all those people—they were dead and buried.

Except for Gabriel.

The best thing Sebastian could do for his brother was stay as far away from him as possible. Gabriel had been left out of the magic world and it had kept him safe.

If he'd just stay out of it now he'll be fine, thought Sebastian. *And I'll do what I set out to.*

Sebastian moved quickly through the trees, trying desperately to escape the tiredness and the biting memories. He kept seeing his grandmother's face as she died and the memory of Elise's pale skin after Malvina had served her poison with a cheerful smile. He had forgotten his parents, his grandparents, and even Gabriel. Of course, it could have all been a spell, but maybe it had been more. Perhaps Sebastian had chosen to forget warmth and kindness--perhaps it made his cruel life easier.

Even though Sebastian was so close to his original goal, so close to bringing the amulet to the ice maiden, he changed direction. *There's time*, he thought. And so, Sebastian chose to let destiny wait, while he took one more visit to the past.

Sebastian made his way through the frosty cemetery. Past the icy gate, the gnarled snow covered tree limbs and the grim gravestones all in a row, he came to the corner of the cemetery where his family lay. He stared down at their names, wondering how different his life would have been if they had lived. What would he have become? Would it have changed his destiny? Would he even have been a sorcerer? Would he have been a murderer? Now, he'd never know.

Sebastian slumped over, suddenly overcome by weakness and emotion. He fell to his knees feeling the familiar call of sleep. The last thing he saw was his mother's name carved into stone. His last thought was both a plea and a question, one he hadn't dared to ask before. *Forgive me?*

Gabriel's dreams were bright and full of different faces. They swirled around him, familiar but difficult to place. An old fisherman and his kind wife, a skinny man with glasses and a sour expression, a golden owl, a broken ship and two women—one made of ice, another with unforgettable eyes—he knew them and yet he didn't. They spun in his mind, vivid and nonsensical. He awoke suddenly to the feeling of being shaken.

"Gabriel—wake up! It's taken me forever to find you!"

Gabriel opened his eyes and saw a familiar face—unfortunately he couldn't remember exactly who the person was.

"Gabriel! You're a sight for sore eyes! I've been trackin' you for so lon' after the storm. It's takin' me this lon' to find you."

"Storm?"

"Aye, don't you remember the terrible storm? You were on my ship...my sister asked me to brin' you? When I awoke in the mornin' I found myself on shore and you were gone. I thought for sure, you'd perished at sea and my sister was goin' to kill me," said Brishen.

The images of a beautiful ship as green as moss, crashing waves and a golden owl all flashed in Gabriel's mind. "I'm sorry...my memories are a bit scattered—I'm recovering from a spell."

"For someone who didn't know much about magic, you certainly get mixed up in it enough."

"I'm starting to remember now. We were on a ship. There was a terrible storm, I thought you died. I was rescued...by..." Gabriel struggled to remember. "By an old fisherman and his wife—they had a little shanty and were so kind to me. Their names were...I can't remember!" exclaimed Gabriel in frustration.

"Is this yours?" Brishen asked, holding up the now infamous chisel. "It was on the ground beside you."

Gabriel grabbed the chisel from Brishen. "Yes—that's my chisel. Sebastian had it. He used it to kill the witch. But how did he get it?"

Brishen pulled Gabriel to standing. "Just slow down, friend, you're not making sense. Work backwards. Think of where you are now and then how you got here.

"The Goblin sent me here. He gave me something." Gabriel put the chisel into one pocket and dug out the shiny compass from another. "He gave me this compass, to help me find my way."

Brishen took it from Gabriel and examined it closely.

"Doesn't seem to be particularly useful to me. All it does is point at you."

"No, no!" replied Gabriel hastily. "It's supposed to point to the strongest magic. It led me to this swamp to find—a medallion and the person who had it last, my brother, Sebastian.

"You have a brother?"

"Yes, a twin brother. Only I forgot him. It was another spell." Gabriel let out a sigh. "It's complicated.

But I must find him. He has the medallion--the one I need to… "

"To?" questioned Brishen.

"To…" Gabriel struggled to remember, then as an artist pieces together the glass in a stained glass window to form an image, all of Gabriel's memories fell into place. "To bring the ice maiden to life. Yes, Brishen, I remember. I remember!" Gabriel shouted happily. Then Gabriel realized who he was speaking to.

"You're alive!" Gabriel hugged Brishen tightly. "I thought you'd died. I was so sure it was my fault. And I was so sure the Gypsy would never forgive me. The Gypsy! How could I have forgotten her? And now when I see her again she won't hate me. This is wonderful!" Gabriel gripped Brishen even tighter.

"Enough there, Gabriel. It sounds like you have a lon' story to tell me and an awful lot to do."

"I have to find Sebastian. He's got the medallion and I don't know what he'll do with it." Gabriel looked down at the compass in his hand, turning left and right, moving in each direction but still the needle pointed squarely at him. "It's supposed to show me the strongest magic, and that should be the medallion. I don't understand this."

"Looks like it thinks you're the strongest magic," answered Brishen.

"That's impossible," replied Gabriel, shaking his head.

"Ah, my friend, haven't you learned by now that nothin' is impossible?"

Gabriel let out a surprisingly loud laugh. "Now you sound like your sister. My brother keeps calling me slow and maybe I am. Nothing is impossible—except figuring out where my brother has gone without this compass working."

"That's where you're wron'," answered Brishen, flashing Gabriel one of his mischievous smiles. He pulled two fingers up to his lips and blew a loud and high whistle. From somewhere in between the trees, Owl emerged. "How do you think I found you? Now what do I tell him we're lookin' for?"

"A man who looks exactly like me—and I do mean exactly. He's wearing a torn black cloak. He knows a lot of magic and he may be hiding."

"You heard Gabriel," Brishen said to the Owl. "Track him and we'll follow." Without hesitation, Owl took to the sky. "The beauty of a golden owl, is he's easy to spot in the sky. We'll follow him on foot while you tell me all these crazy stories you've been jabberin' about. And slowly, you had my head spinnin' back there."

"After all your long stories, it seems only fair I return the favor," Gabriel answered.

Brishen let out a laugh. "I suppose I deserve that. Now start from the beginning." The two men began walking through the woods, keeping track of a gold owl in the sky.

"I guess the beginning is when I found this old cave—no, I'm wrong. The beginning was when my brother and I were four years old." Gabriel began his story, with a heavy heart for the sad things he'd witnessed, and a strong hope that he could somehow make things right.

Sebastian awoke shivering. He lay upon his mother's grave and wondered what he was doing there. He was so close to finishing, so close to bringing the ice maiden to life, why had he stopped? Gabriel might already be awake and following him! Hurriedly, Sebastian stood, gave the four graves a quick look then rushed out of the cemetery and toward the cave where he knew the ice maiden would be waiting.

He felt the medallion, heavy around his neck. It had taken so much from him and now—now he'd get his repayment. It was far too late for things like sadness and forgiveness. He'd bring the ice maiden to life and complete his greatest spell. And heaven help Gabriel if he got in his way.

After all, thought Sebastian, *I survived losing him once, I'm sure I can survive it again.*

"Gabriel, I think Owl's spotted him!" called Brishen. The two men stared at the pieces of sky they could see between the tree branches and the golden owl moving briskly across it. "We need to keep goin' right, just down this ravine."

"Right?" asked Gabriel. "That's the way to the Frozen Forest—that's the way home."

Home, thought Gabriel. How strange the word seemed now. What did it mean? He'd seen so much, met so many people, remembered so many things he hadn't realized he'd forgotten. And now he found that he still had family left in the world. How different it would be to go back.? And the ice maiden, what of her? Was he following Sebastian to gain the medallion, or because he didn't want to lose his brother again?

Brishen and Gabriel traveled on, and the woods became more familiar to Gabriel. The green leaves changed to dark barren branches and cold winds swept through the woods.

"Home certainly isn't the most welcomin' place for you is it?" asked Brishen.

"Before, I never thought about it. Never thought about what it was like to be anywhere else."

"And now?"

"Now, I'm starting to realize that being in a certain place for a very long time doesn't make it your home."

Hearing the sadness in Gabriel's voice, Brishen quickly changed the subject. "So, where do you think this magician brother of yours is headin' to?"

"My cabin—I mean our cabin. Where we grew up. He must have been there while I was gone. He had my chisel and that's where he must have, wait—my chisel—it couldn't be…"

"Couldn't be what?" asked Brishen.

"That he wants the medallion for the same reason I do."

"What? There are two of you crazy enough to try to brin' a block of ice to life?"

"He had the chisel, he's heading that way—he keeps talking about unfinished business. That cave, it's the same one our grandmother hid him in, when we were little. He must have found her! I have to hurry."

"I tell you Gabe, this better be the most beautiful ice woman in all the world."

Gabriel gave Brishen a serious look, "This might be dangerous."

"Hell's bells! A sailor always welcomes an adventure, danger be damned!" said Brishen in his cheerful way.

"I put you in harm's way once and you almost died doing me a favor. I won't repay that kindness by getting you killed. I have to go the rest of the way on my own."

"That's fool talk—I can help you— "

"I know you can, but this is my fight, my quest. You've been a good friend, but I know in my heart I have to do this on my own."

"If it's dangerous, all the more reason I should come," Brishen argued.

"I don't think my brother will kill me, he had the chance more than once and didn't take it. But that doesn't mean he'll spare you. I need to do this alone. Besides, I'll need someone to help me if he decides to turn me into a toad."

Brishen laughed. "If he does, I'll have to keep Owl away from you." He let out a heavy sigh. "For an easy goin' guy you can be pretty stubborn. Just in case you lose track, I'm going to let Owl keep followin' your brother."

"Thanks, I appreciate it."

"No need to thank me. There's one last thin' and I know I'm riskin' death by doin' it, but do you want to know my sister's name? Just in case anythin' should go wron'—I think she'd want you to know."

"No. I'll ask her myself when this is done. I made her a promise that I'd see her again and it's one I intend to keep."

Brishen nodded his head. "I understand. Safe journey, Gabe. 'Til we meet again."

Gabriel nodded back. "'Til we meet again." With that, Brishen turned back and Gabriel continued on, heading back to the cave and to his destiny.

Gabriel made it to the cave just as sunset was flittering through the trees. It cast an eerie glow through the Frozen Forest and made the ice that covered all the trees shine a bloody red.

Gabriel stood in front of the entrance to the cave, wondering what awaited him. Was Sebastian there? Had he managed to bring the ice maiden to life? And if powerful magic had a great cost, what had Sebastian paid?

He stepped into the cavern and followed the snaking tunnel. He pulled the chisel out of his cloak pocket, holding it out in front of him like a weapon.

Gabriel rounded the sharp corner and came to the wide-open space, and the beautiful and immobile ice maiden. The light of sunset reflected through the openings in the top of the cavern, making it seem as though she were being consumed by flame.

Gabriel stared at her. She was as he remembered— striking, but cold and unreachable. He scanned the space, looking for Sebastian, but he was alone in the cave. He noticed something just beyond the statue and against the wall. He kneeled to the ground and picked up his fiddle and the bow that lay nearby.

"It's still here." The wood felt so cold against Gabriel's hands, but once he touched the instrument, a pang of longing pulsed through him so strong, he staggered. He shut his eyes, overwhelmed by a rush of images: his mother and father, his grandparents and Sebastian— so much had been lost. Almost by their own volition, Gabriel's hands brought the violin up to his chin.

The song was sad, but instead of being colored by despair, it was filled with hope. Music as a light in the darkness, as a shield against the grief, as a way to change his story. Gabriel lost himself in it, and didn't hear the loud hooing coming from outside of the cave, or the footsteps through the tunnel. He didn't even notice Sebastian as he emerged from around the corner.

For a moment Sebastian listened and watched as his brother was lost in the music. It was like watching himself in a dream, a vision of himself playing a fiddle. His mother had played—he remembered now. She'd shown him how the strings made sounds, and let him pluck each one. He'd forgotten how beautiful simple things could be. Then he saw the ice maiden, still perfect and still waiting.

"It looks like I'm late for the celebration," Sebastian said. Gabriel dropped the violin and before he could utter a single word, another voice interrupted.

"No, my dear boy. You're right on time." Standing next to the statue was the same robed figure from Sebastian's memory, the same figure that had killed his grandmother. Two thin, bony hands pushed back the cloak hood and there was the face of the Swamp Witch.

Gabriel let out a small gasp. "Sebastian killed you. I saw it."

The woman let out a terrible laugh. "You act as though he hasn't killed me before."

"That's not the Swamp Witch!" Sebastian called out. "She speaks in rhyme."

"Ah, my clever boy. Yes, I borrowed her body for a bit back in the swamp. She's quite useful, but I must tell you that speaking in rhyme is quite a bother. I think if I had to speak that way all the time, I'd strangle myself." She ran her bluish hands over her cheeks. "Perhaps you know this face better?"

In a moment, her hair grew from seaweed green to spiderweb gray, and her bluish face turned pale with deep lines and age spots. Her eyes darkened from gray to the blackest black. It was Malvina, the woman who'd raised Sebastian, the one who'd killed his parents, his grandmother, the girl who was his best friend, the one who'd forced him to be separated from his brother, and the first person he'd murdered.

"You're dead," said Sebastian, his voice not sounding as steady as he wanted. "I stabbed you through the heart and watched you die."

"Ah, my dear Sebastian, you always did amuse. Did you really think you could kill me? That a simple knife would do *me* in? It was laughable really. I knew I had to get you to leave town—to find my medallion—but that ridiculous girl made you want to stay, made you want to give up dark magic. She made you weak, and a pathetic little thing she was too. What was her name again? Eleanor?"

"Elise." Sebastian replied his voice almost a growl.

"Yes, of course." The figure laughed. "It was all so easy---slip her a little poison—and make sure you knew it was me that killed your little love. Making a poor, lonely, desperate boy think he killed me, so he'd run off and do my dirty work for me. The one thing I hadn't counted on was that amulet doing such a thorough job of hiding you from me for so many years. You always find a way to be a problem, Sebastian. I must say it's gotten quite tiring. But it turns out, I didn't need you after all. Once good old Silas died, the spell he used to hide your brother died along with him. I can't tell you how excited I was to go looking for *you* and find a much better version---one so much easier to manipulate."

Malvina's face changed, becoming a flesh and blood replica of the statue next to her. "I have to say Gabriel, you did a wonderful job. It's quite an amazing face. It's by far the loveliest I've ever come across. I think I'll use it from now on. It's amazing how much people fall all over themselves to help you when you're beautiful. Look how well it worked with both of you? Think of all you both did, just for this face."

Gabriel never thought he could feel such loathing for the ice maiden's face.

"Enough with this pathetic monologue. You've always enjoyed listening to your own voice. Since this is what you want..." Sebastian pulled the medallion from around his neck, dangling it in front of the witch. "Come and get it."

"She can't." Gabriel replied and walked over to stand shoulder to shoulder with his brother. "She had the medallion in the swamp, had it for a good long time. If that's all she wanted, this would be over by now."

She let out another cackling laugh. "Gabriel you do surprise me—over and over again. Clearly I chose the wrong brother all those years ago. You do know this whole splendid adventure—everything has been about you. It took a while for Silas' magic to stop protecting you. I was impressed that it even lasted a bit after his death. It's a shame. If I'd known of your existence sooner—perhaps there'd have been a lot less death. Then again, killing is such sport, I doubt I'd have been able to stop myself."

Her beautiful face widened into an awful grin. "You've been the missing piece this entire time. You see, it started with a prophecy. That a child born on the seventh day of the seventh month, under the seventh full moon, would have the power to find and control the amulet. As you've noticed it tends to get a bit, how shall we say, unpredictable. But imagine if you could truly harness that kind of power. The things that you could do, or undo. You'd be a god. It was a treasure worth waiting for, and you can't imagine how long I spent waiting for you. When I stole Sebastian I thought I had succeeded. But I realized, he's only half of the whole—the spell needs both of you to work."

"You had us in the swamp. Why didn't you cast the spell then?" asked Sebastian.

"Ah, my foolish little ones. Everything was about getting you both here."

"Here, where you killed our grandmother?" asked Gabriel.

"No, where you were born—tonight is the seventh day of the seventh month and there's a full moon dotting the sky. " She let out a loud cackle, "Happy Birthday, dear boys."

"I'd take my own life before I helped you get anything you wanted." Sebastian spit out.

"I wouldn't expect any less bravado from you, Sebastian. Always having to prove your stronger and better than everyone, especially me. But what if gave you want most in all the world? Wouldn't that be a fair exchange?" With that the statue changed. The ice turned pink and warm, changing to flesh and blood. The maiden's features grew smaller and daintier and suddenly she was the lost and sweet Elise.

"Sebastian! I've missed you so much, it's been so long, so very long. We can run away together, just like we talked about."

"Lies!" screamed Sebastian. "All Lies!" Sebastian wouldn't look at her. He couldn't bear to see her again.

"With that amulet," Malvina said, "I can have power over death itself. It's not a lie. I can bring her back to you and give you anything else you desire."

"It's just a trick 'Bastian. She'll kill us as soon as she's through with us."

"And how about you, my darling Gabriel? The lovely Elise's skin grew darker, her eyes changed to a startling blue and green and her hair grew long and dark. She'd changed to Gabriel's Gypsy.

"Gabriel, I've been waiting for you. You said you'd come back. Please hurry, we can be together and it will be wonderful."

"Don't seem so surprised, Gabriel. I've been watching you—checking in from time to time, making sure you were on your way. You do know your precious Gypsy is trapped. A Gypsy who can't wander is quite comical really. The irony of it is absolutely poetic, except that part about falling in love. I hate spells with silly out clauses. It's pointless if you give them a way out." She snorted in disgust.

"Love clause?" Gabriel asked.

She laughed. "Oh, I guess she didn't tell. She needs to fall in love and be loved in return and all that pathetic rot, including the declarations of love, then she's free. Such a silly old-fashioned spell some pathetic journeyman put on her, but you can't expect much from amateurs. Now I can free your sweetheart and you both can ride off into the sunset, or I can kill her," she finished coldly.

"Stay away from her! Stay away or.." Gabriel screamed, pulling the chisel from his pocket.

"Or?" Malvina laughed the sound as harsh as breaking glass. "You'll stab me with your little chisel? That didn't kill me when your brother tried it, but feel free to give it another attempt. Just don't hurt yourself, at least not till I'm done with you."

"And how do we know you won't kill us as soon as you've gotten what you want?" Gabriel asked.

"Because you both have decent enough power--- you'd make excellent minions. I can't be everywhere all the time. Every evil sorceress needs a few strong henchmen. Tell you what boys, since I like you both so very much, I'll sweeten the deal. Not only will you get your lovely ladies, I'll give you back your precious family."

"What?" asked Sebastian.

"Your whiny parents, your pathetic grandparents— you can have them all back. Just one big, boring family."

"And we'd be at your mercy eternally," said Sebastian. "You forget I've lived with you and I know exactly what that entails."

Malvina let out a loud, horrible laugh that echoed against the cave walls. "That sounds like the beginning of a negotiation. What did you have in mind?"

"Our family—and friends—everyone we love will be immune to your magic and your spells. You won't be able to harm any of us, or order us to be harmed. If you do, you'll lose your power entirely."

Malvina cackled. "I knew you'd see the opportunity I could offer you."

Sebastian placed his palm out to offer the amulet to Malvina.

"No!" Gabriel shouted as he slammed into Sebastian, knocking him to the ground. "They wouldn't want this!" Sebastian still held tight to the medallion while Gabriel held his chisel.

"You have to trust me!" Sebastian shouted. "This is the only way!"

They rolled on the ground struggling, when Sebastian fell on top of Gabriel. A sticky wetness covered Gabriel's arm where he still held the chisel. In horror, he looked down, to see it buried in Sebastian's chest. Sebastian fell to the side, blood flowing from his wound. "No!" Gabriel cried, "Please No!" Gabriel fell beside his brother. Bright red blood covered his hands and the icy cavern floor, as Gabriel desperately trying to stop the bleeding.

"Enough playtime!" shouted Malvina and with a toss of her hand she sent Gabriel flying across the icy ground. She kneeled beside the dying sorcerer. "It's time now, darling. Time to finish this."

"I couldn't agree with you more," Sebastian whispered hoarsely. He opened the palm of his hand and held out the blood-covered amulet. He knew he'd have just one chance, one chance for success. Malvina plucked the medallion from his hand. Now that she was holding it, he summoned all his power and shouted, *"Thoghairm úinéir muince."* The sound reverberated against the cavern walls.

Just like in the swamp, Gabriel knew what the spell meant—it summoned the owner of the medallion. Gabriel moved quickly to Sebastian's side. Sebastian grabbed his brother's hand and whispered hoarsely. "Gabriel, repeat what I said—say it, quickly."

"Thoghairm úinéir muince," Gabriel answered.

A wind whipped itself through the cave and a black figure that seemed to be comprised of nothing more than shadow appeared between Malvina and the men.

A look of pure terror crossed Malvina's face. She opened her mouth to scream, but no sound came out. Then Malvina began to change. Her skin bubbled, then melted off, like lava down a volcano. Underneath emerged a gray and feeble woman, as ancient as a an elven ruin. With a crackling sound, she burst into flame and disintegrated into ash. The ashes flew through the air into a steady stream and disappeared into the medallion.

The shadow turned to face the two brothers on the floor—one living and one near death.

As before, the shadow spoke without sound and instead the words formed in their two minds. *Sebastian, you have kept your promise and returned my amulet. For this I am indebted to you. I will grant you one wish. Whatever you desire will be yours.*

"Use it to save yourself," Gabriel cried out aloud.

"No," Sebastian coughed.

"What!"

"I have a chance now. A chance to put right the terrible things I've done. Please Gabriel, I need to do this." Sebastian turned his head to address the dark spirit. "Long ago, when I first found that amulet, I used it to call a giant wave that killed dozens of men. I want to undo it. I want to undo the damage."

You wish to undo the damage the amulet caused? the shadow asked.

"Yes," Sebastian coughed out.

When the night is done and the first rays of the sun kiss the sky, your wish will be granted.

Without a single flutter, the shadow was quite suddenly gone.

"I'm so sorry Bastian. I never wanted to hurt you. You can't die. Please. Isn't there a spell, you could try? Tell me the words, I'll do my best," Gabriel begged as he held his brother's hand.

"No, Gabriel. Magic can destroy you." Sebastian felt coldness creep in and clung to the warmth of his brother's hand. "None of this is your fault, I had to be convincing to trick Malvina and it worked. It's enough for me that I finally stopped her and you have a chance to live in peace." Sebastian coughed. "Go back to the girl you love and live a good life. Be happy, for both of us." Sebastian squeezed his brother's hand one last time, then shut his eyes. His head fell back and he was gone.

"Come back!" Gabriel sobbed. "Come back!" Gabriel shook his brother violently as though to rouse him from sleep. "Come back!" He reached down and pulled the chisel from his brother's chest, his hands covered in blood. "Don't leave me!" Hot tears poured down his face. He took the chisel to the Ice Maiden and with an inhuman shout began to chip away at her. He stabbed and stabbed until there was nothing left that resembled a maiden. Gabriel looked down at his hands, covered in his brother's blood and at the lump of lifeless ice, and fell to his knees and sobbed.

"What the hell kind of story is this!" Casper exclaimed, sitting up in bed.

"Why would you tell us this," Johanna asked, trying not to let the tears that had formed in the corner of her eyes escape. "Are you just trying to be mean?"

"Now Johanna, the story isn't over—" Mrs. Kinder interjected.

"It's a bad story! And you're a bad lady for telling it!" Casper said.

"Now Casper, you're taking this too much to heart—" Mrs. Kinder said.

"Casper's right. It's an awful story and I don't want to hear any more." Johanna replied.

"Me neither." Casper answered and plopped himself back down on the bed, turning his back on Mrs. Kinder.

"Now children—"

"No, we're done now. It's time to sleep." Johanna said firmly. Then she turned her back on Mrs. Kinder.

"Are you sure you really don't want to know what happens next?"

"We're tired. Just leave us alone." Johanna said coldly, while Casper remained silent.

"Okay children, try to get some rest."

After Mrs. Kinder had turned off the light and left the room, Casper asked, "Johanna, why does everyone have to die?"

Johanna put her arm around her little brother, "I don't know, Casper, but Dad will be fine. You'll see. And no matter what we have each other." Johanna listened quietly while Casper's breathing became heavy and even, so she knew he was asleep.

Only then did she finally let the tears she'd been holding back escape. She couldn't help but think about Casper's question. W*hy does everyone have to die?* With tears and that sad question echoing in her mind, Johanna fell into a bleak slumber that even dreams wouldn't visit.

When the children awoke the next day, Mrs. Kinder was gone and in her place was their mother, Emily.

"Hey, sleepyheads. It's time to get up," their mother called out to them, "I made blueberry pancakes."

When the blurry eyed children made their way downstairs, they were greeted by a set kitchen table and a stack of blueberry pancakes on a white platter.

"My favorite!" Casper exclaimed wide-eyed. It'd been some time since the Sullivan household had been served freshly made pancakes.

Casper hurriedly pulled out a chair to sit and began heaping pancakes onto his plate.

"Leave some for your sister," his mother told him.

Johanna eyed the plate suspiciously. "Do we have time for this? Aren't we going to be late for school?"

"School—schmool." Casper chimed in with his mouth full of maple syrup and pancake.

"You're not going today," Emily answered.

"What?" Casper's eyes grew bigger. "Is it Christmas? Or is this some kind of a joke?" Casper's eyes narrowed.

"Neither. Your Dad is well enough to have visitors, so we're going to the hospital this morning, so eat up and then get changed."

"Dad's better!" Casper exclaimed again, his mouth still full of pancake and syrup.

"Your dad is *doing* better," Emily answered carefully. "He's not leaving the hospital anytime soon, but it's okay for you both to see him now. And he really misses you guys."

Not as much as I miss him. Johanna thought but didn't answer. She got up from the table. "I'm going to go get dressed."

"But you haven't had any pancakes," Emily said.

"Casper can have the rest of mine, I'm not hungry. I'm just going to get ready."

"Me too!" Casper exclaimed then jumped from his chair. "Dad's better!" he shouted as he rushed up the steps.

In response, Johanna and Emily both had the very same thought: *I hope so.*

The hospital smelled funny to Johanna, like rubbing alcohol and Lysol. And her sneakers creaked on the linoleum, reminding her of the whine Mrs. Kinder's front door makes. Casper was oddly quiet and gave no protest at all when holding his mother's hand (which was quite an unusual occurrence).

Johanna eyed the nurses with their clipboards as they spoke to each other about Mr. Ribinowitz who wouldn't take his medicine and Mrs. Carlisle who refused to eat anything until they let her poodle Felix in to see her. *I wonder if they talk about my dad too?* Johanna thought.

The children followed their mother, to the door with their father's name written on a white board. "Heinrich Klaus Sullivan" looked so formal and strange to Johanna. Even other grown-ups just called him Henry. But most important, he was Dad to Casper and Johanna.

Henry gave his children a warm smile as they walked in the door. His black hair was a bit disheveled and he looked paler than Johanna ever remembered him being, but his blue eyes still had their welcoming glow.

"If it isn't Joey and my personal friendly ghost. You wouldn't believe how much I missed you both. Come sit by me."

Casper hesitated while Johanna moved slowly. Both children couldn't help but stare at the various tubes attached to their Dad, and the strange machines that beeped and whined next do his bed.

"Come on now, don't be nervous. They're just some silly wires the doctors use to watch me. Now come here!"

Casper and Johanna walked right up to the edge of the bed and stood immobile. "You guys can't be afraid of your old Dad, come sit."

"I don't want to break you, Daddy," said Casper softly as he sat on the very edge of the bed with Johanna right next to him.

Henry Sullivan kissed the top of his head. "No worries, champ—I promise you won't." Henry reached his arm out toward Johanna and pulled her in a half hug, and gave her a kiss as well. "I missed you guys so much. Tell me what you've been doing? How's school?"

"Fine," Johanna answered.

"Boring," replied Casper.

"Oh c'mon, something interesting had to have happened. Did you learn anything new?"

I learned how to be as quiet as humanly possible, so people don't ask me questions about you, Johanna thought, but didn't say aloud, and instead answered, "Not really. We read a lot of books about boys growing up. I keep waiting for them to give us some girl books, but they never do. It's always boys with horses, or boys fishing, or boys getting shipwrecked."

"That's cause boys are way more fun." Casper answered smugly.

"Ah Casper, you'll be changing your mind on that soon enough," Mr. Sullivan answered with a smile and rumpled Casper's hair.

Emily moved from her spot across the room to sit in the chair on the other side of the bed from Johanna and Casper. She gave the three of them a small smile.

"So when do you get out of here?" Casper asked. "When can you come home?"

"Not exactly sure, buddy. I have one more surgery, then I have to rest. After that I should be home."

"*Another* surgery," Casper whined. "You just had one."

"It can be a little complicated sometimes, but I'll be home before you know it."

I already know you're gone. How much longer do you need? Johanna thought. "How long can we stay?" Johanna asked suddenly.

Mr. Sullivan looked at his wife. "I think we bargained the nurses for two hours."

"That's not enough time," Casper whined again, leaning into his dad a bit.

"We'll have all the time in the world when I get home," said Mr. Sullivan.

If you come home, thought Johanna.

"So you just lie around all day?" Casper asked.

Mr. Sullivan laughed. "Most of the time. Sometimes they let me watch TV. Plus your mom comes in and reads to me when she can."

"Why does everyone like to read so much? Movies are so much easier."

"Easier isn't always better," Henry Sullivan responded. "And I think sometimes what we imagine is better than what any movie could come up with."

"I don't know," Casper answered, unconvinced.

"What do you think, Johanna?" asked their father.

"I think it depends on the story. Some stories just aren't worth it."

Mr. Sullivan gave Johanna a puzzled look and asked, "Like what?"

"Well, really sad ones—or ones where awful things happen. Like in the story Mrs. Kinder was telling us."

"Yeah!" Casper chimed in. "It was terrible—well there were a few cool parts, like when this dragon exploded, but mostly it was bad. Like everyone dies in it. Who wants to read that?"

"I find it hard to believe Mrs. Kinder told you a story where *everyone* dies?" chimed in Emily Sullivan.

"Well, she did." Johanna answered. "Or at least most everyone died."

"The story ended with *everyone* dying?" Mr. Sullivan asked.

"Yes—well, no. It didn't actually *end* that way," Johanna answered.

"We made her stop telling it when people just kept dying," Casper added.

"Ah well, now I see your mistake. You can't really judge a story until you finish it." Mr. Sullivan answered. "If you don't know the ending, how can you decide if it's happy or sad, or even worthwhile?"

"But if everyone dies, what's the point?" Johanna asked.

Mr. Sullivan took a second to answer, and his voice took on a strangely lullaby-like tone. "Sooner or later, everyone dies, Johanna. But people are more than that—and their stories are more than that. There are some things much bigger than death."

"Like what?" Casper asked.

"Like love," Emily Sullivan answered, reaching over to squeeze her husband's hand.

"Yes, like love." Mr. Sullivan replied, taking his wife's hand and giving it a quick kiss. He turned to his children. "Why, if it weren't for love I wouldn't be me and neither of you would be you."

"What?" Johanna asked puzzled, while Casper just gave his father a suspicious look.

"Now, I must of told you both the story of your great grandparents Liesel and Patrick?"

"Just that they met, when great grandfather went to Germany with the army, and they got married and came to live together in America." Johanna answered.

"That's all I told you?" Mr. Sullivan asked.

"That's all I remember," Johanna responded.

"Well, it's because of Great grandmother Liesel that we got our names."

"You mean it's her fault I'm named after some stupid ghost?"

Both Mr. and Mrs. Sullivan laughed. "Casper I've told you time and time again, you aren't named after a ghost," said Emily.

"You see, your great grandmother Liesel—she loved her homeland, but she loved your great grandfather Patrick even more, so she was willing to leave Germany behind and make a home in America, just to be with him. She had one condition, however." Henry Sullivan paused dramatically as he often did when telling a particularly interesting story.

"Which was?" Johanna asked.

"That if she had to leave behind Germany, that all her children and great grandchildren and great great grandchildren be given traditional German names. She had one son named Klaus and another she named Casper, after her own father."

"There were *more* Caspers?" Casper asked incredulously.

Henry Sullivan laughed. "Lots more."

"What about me? Were there other Johannas?" Johanna asked.

"One other that I know of. Liesel had a twin sister named Johanna, who died during the war. Liesel never stopped missing Johanna and she never had any daughters to pass the name on to. She made her sons promise if they had girls, they'd name them after their Aunt Johanna, but neither one of them did. My papa made me promise the same thing, and you are the first Sullivan girl born since then, and thus the next Johanna." Mr. Sullivan finished with a twinkle in his eye.

"But everyone just agreed to do what great-grandmother Liesel's wanted?" Johanna asked, looking at her mother. "Didn't you want to choose your own names?"

"It seemed the right thing to do," Emily responded. "And when you were born, you just seemed exactly like a Johanna—and Casper, well, he was pale just like a ghost, so that fit too," Emily ended with a wink.

"I knew it." Casper answered, his eyes narrowing. "It's always been about a ghost, hasn't it?"

"What was the old Johanna like?" Johanna asked.

"From what I heard she used to tell stories and paint pictures about them. And supposedly she and Liesel had their own secret language no one else could understand. And it was said that Johanna had this really infectious laugh, that once she started laughing, everyone else couldn't help laughing either."

"What about the other Caspers?" Casper asked.

"Well the only one I know about is my Uncle Casper. He loved to bake—"

"Bake?" Casper echoed, with disgust and Johanna couldn't help but laugh.

"He also liked to make models of kinds, but particularly ships in bottles—"

"Like pirate ships?" Casper asked, suddenly excited.

"Sometimes."

"Woohoo—Uncle Casper was a pirate!" Casper sang out.

"That's not what Dad said—" Johanna interjected.

Henry Sullivan shook his head and laughed. "You never know."

The Sullivan family continued to laugh and talk. Johanna relaxed and felt felt that the world could go back to normal. Then she would notice the beeping machines her father was still attached to and she wondered if even the word "normal" had changed.

Finally Emily looked down at her wristwatch. "Well kids, I'm afraid it's time for your Dad to rest."

"Already?" Casper whined.

"Afraid so." Emily answered.

"I want a good solid hug from both of you before you leave." Henry Sullivan said with pretended sternness.

Casper leaned over and gave his Dad a hug. "Hurry up and come home." Then got up off the bed to wait by the doorway.

Johanna leaned over and gave her father a hug.

"Don't worry Joey, everything will be fine."

Johanna couldn't stop herself from asking, "But what if it isn't?"

"I promise, one way or another it will be," and with that Henry Sullivan kissed his daughter goodbye.

Johanna and Casper were both quiet on the ride home. Johanna couldn't help thinking about what her father had said about stories and love. It was nagging at her now that she hadn't let Mrs. Kinder finish her story. Maybe it would still be terrible and sad, but what if it wasn't? What if Gabriel could end up happy, even if he had lost his brother?

"Mom, is Mrs. Kinder going to watch us tomorrow when Dad's in surgery?" Johanna asked.

"That was the plan," Emily responded.

"No!" Casper whined. "She'll just keep torturing us."

"Oh stop that Casper. She wasn't *that* bad," said Johanna.

Casper's eyes narrowed. "So you've turned on me now. I see how it is," he answered and became quite suddenly, and sullenly, quiet.

"I think Dad was right and we should hear the end of her story. Besides she was nice to us and we were kinda mean the other night."

Casper gave Johanna no response and instead just continued to glare at her.

"Good, then it's settled, you'll spend the day with Mrs. Kinder," said Emily.

Casper let out a deep sigh. Johanna, on the other hand, felt the faint stirrings of something she hadn't felt in a long time—a feeling that had a strange resemblance to hope.

"Hello children, you both look well," said Mrs. Kinder as she ushered them into her home. "I thought today we might make some cookies. I found an old recipe for some spritz cookies."

"Spit cookies?" Casper asked in horror.

Mrs. Kinder let out a laugh. "No, *spritz* cookies. There is no saliva involved, I assure you—just large quantities of butter. I have a little press that makes them into shapes. I was going to make some flowers, I thought they might be nice to bring to my church quilting circle. You both can help."

"Church?" Casper echoed. "Are they aware you are using us as slave labor?"

"Casper!" Johanna exclaimed. "I don't think an afternoon of baking cookies is the same as working in a sweatshop. Besides you're named after great Uncle Casper who liked baking *so much*, so this should be right up your alley."

"He was a PIRATE! The baking thing was a COV-ER."

"Sure, sure," answered Johanna.

Mrs. Kinder escorted the children into the kitchen and in no time at all had them settle d in at the kitchen table in front of several ceramic bowls. Both children were wearing aprons.

"Did I have to get the one with the red cherries on it?" Casper whined. "Isn't baking girlie enough?"

"Well, if you want the pink roses Johanna has or the kittens I'm wearing, I'm sure we could accommodate you," Mrs. Kinder answered cheerfully.

In response, Johanna stifled a laugh and Casper grumbled out "Nevermind."

Mrs. Kinder instructed the children on how much to measure and when they were ready showed them how to load the "cookie gun." The word gun excited Casper, who had finally found an aspect to baking that he deemed respectable for boys. "Now this must have been what great Uncle Casper was into," he said excitedly. "I just wish we had cooler shapes besides flowers? Don't you have any skull and crossbones?" He asked Mrs. Kinder.

"Sorry Casper dear, fresh out," answered Mrs. Kinder. Johanna laughed.

Mrs. Kinder showed Casper and Johanna how to manipulate the metal cylinder and press the cookies, and they spent the next hour pressing the dough into the shape of flowers.

"So what's this I hear about a great Uncle Casper?" Mrs. Kinder asked as she placed a cookie tray into the oven.

"Our Dad told us about him, and our great grand-mother Liesel who gave us all German names," Casper answered.

"You know I met your great grandmother Liesel when I was a little girl."

Johanna's eyes widened, "How?"

"My parents had brought me to visit my Aunt Adelaide who was ill—she lived in this house before we did. Liesel was a good friend of Adelaide and volun-teered to watch me one afternoon while they took dear Auntie to the doctor."

"What was she like?" Johanna asked.

"Oh, very nice from what I remember. She had a perfume that smelled like oranges and flowers. She made me some tea and we had little party. She told me I reminded her of her sister."

"Did she tell you anything about her?" Johanna asked.

"She said 'Johanna told the best stories of anyone she'd ever known', and then she told me one of them."

Johanna felt a prickle on the back of her neck. "That wouldn't be the same story you were telling us before?"

"Perhaps, or perhaps not. But you both didn't want to finish it, so it doesn't matter." Mrs. Kinder answered as she finished stacking the dirty dishes in the sink.

"We want to hear it," Johanna answered. "And we're sorry we got mad the other night. You're not a terrible person."

Mrs. Kinder smiled. "How about you Casper, can you stand to hear more?"

Casper narrowed his eyes a bit and said "You have a cookie gun—so I'll trust you—*this* time."

Mrs. Kinder laughed, "Thank you for that enthusiastic vote of confidence, Casper dear. Now since you both are ready to finish our story, it's seems foolish not to get started. Let's head into the sitting room and pick up where we left off.

The sun had set and the sitting room was dark. Mrs. Kinder had once again retrieved the mysterious golden book, and was sitting in the chair across from the children. She opened the drawer in the side table next to her, pulled out a box of matches, and lit the hurricane lamp perched on it. The light cast odd shadows around the room that reminded Johanna of a storybook picture of imps dancing round a fire.

"Don't you have any *real* lights?" Casper whined.

Mrs. Kinder gave a small laugh. "Not only are these kind of lamps economical, but I think they create just the right ambiance for our story."

"Ambiance?" Casper asked.

"It means that it creates a special sort of mood." Mrs. Kinder answered.

"Is it bright enough for you to be able to see the book?" Johanna asked.

"I'm right next to the lamp and with my glasses I'll do just fine. Now where were we?

"It was awful—Sebastian had just died, the ice maiden was destroyed and Gabriel was heartbroken," said Johanna.

Mrs. Kinder adjusted her spectacles to peer at Johanna. "You're quite right that is an awful part, but you'd be quite surprised how often wonderful things start out as awful ones. Now, we've been quite neglectful in leaving the story at such a disturbing moment, so we'd best hurry back and see if there's not a bit of wonderful left to find."

Gabriel sat in the darkness of the cave. Malvina was dead, but so was Sebastian, and the Ice Maiden who had started this terrible journey was destroyed beyond recognition. He'd failed at bringing the her to life, failed at saving his brother, failed at being a hero. Failed.

He picked up the violin and bow, but couldn't play. Instead, he held them to his chest as though they could soothe his aching heart. He felt cold and empty, as though he were as dead along with Sebastian; like half of him was gone, and the remaining half was broken beyond repair.

In a few minutes, a hint of sunlight reached into the cave. That was when things began to change. First, all the ice began to melt and the air turned warmer. The light grew brighter until the cave was filled with it.

Then, Sebastian's wound began to heal and the blood vanished. Sebastian let out a cough.

"Bastian you're alive!" Gabriel cried, grabbing Sebastian and holding onto him tightly.

"Not if you keep grabbing me like that." Sebastian answered. "What's going on?"

"Everything's changing."

"What do you mean?" Sebastian asked sitting up.

"You were dead. Now you're alive! The ice is melting, everything's warm." Gabriel responded, his voice full of joy. "It must be your wish."

"But how? I just wished for those men to be alive. How would that change all this?"

Sebastian stared in wonder at the melting ice.

"No, you wished for the damage the amulet made to be undone," Gabriel said.

Gabriel helped Sebastian stand. Then the two brothers rushed out of the cave together.

"It's not possible!" Sebastian exclaimed.

"It can't be." Gabriel said with amazement as he gazed around at the forest. It was no longer frozen, but warm and full of leafy trees and birds chirping.

"What if they're alive?" Sebastian asked.

"What if *who's* alive?" Gabriel answered.

"Everyone."

The pair quickly ran back to the old cottage. It wasn't a cold weatherworn cabin anymore, but the charming, warm cottage from their childhood.

"Boys! You're back! A voice called from inside the house." Margarite emerged from the doorway. "My boys, so grown up, but still out wreaking havoc together."

"Mother!" they said in unison as they walked up to her and enveloped her in their arms.

"Such a lucky mother I am, to have two wonderful boys who love me so much. Can you both stay for supper? Your father should be home soon. Oh, but Sebastian, I'm sure Elise is waiting for you."

"Elise?" Sebastian replied.

"Yes, Elise—you know, your *wife*, Elise." Margarite responded.

"Wife?" Sebastian said, a newfound hope in his voice.

"Are you ill, dear?"

"No, Mother, he's not, he's just playing a little joke on you. Of course, he needs to get back to his wife. And I'll take him back there, right now, if you can remind me where his house is." Gabriel said.

"Where his house is? Gabriel, you live there! At least you live there now. I don't know where you live when you're off traveling. You remember the lovely little stone cottage near the edge of town? With all the roses around it? You boys really need to stop with these pranks, you're much too old for them."

"Yes, mother you're absolutely right," Sebastian agreed.

"And how are grandfather and grandmother doing?" Gabriel asked.

"Oh they're having a lovely time visiting the lowlands. They should be back in a fortnight or so."

Gabriel grinned at Sebastian and Sebastian actually smiled back.

"That's wonderful. We really should be going, but we'll come back and see you soon. Please give Father our love." Gabriel said.

"Of course." She gave them each a kiss on their cheek. "Oh wait, hold on—I have some teacakes for you. Margarite ran into the house and returned with a basket. "Take these home with you. You're not so old yet that I can't spoil you." They each kissed her again and set off to town.

"I'm married," said Sebastian in amazement. "Elise is alive. This has to be a dream. No one gets this kind of a second chance."

Gabriel laughed. "No one except for you—or us, that is. And I have to say that marriage has mellowed you out. To think, just hours ago you were an arrogant know-it-all sorcerer with murderous tendencies."

"Don't get too cocky, I'm still older and wiser than you." The pair wandered through the town, amazed at the warmth and prosperity that filled it.

"I think that's the place," said Sebastian dryly. There was a stone cottage, surrounded by ivy and red roses, but the amazing thing was the statue in the front yard. Carved in stone was a woman, an exact replica of the Ice Maiden. She stood on a pedestal in which one simple word was carved. "Hope."

"You're home," a female voice called from the doorway.

"Elise!" Sebastian called out as he ran to her. He swung her up into his arms and kissed her. The sort of kiss that people slay dragons for, or come at the end of long and difficult quests—but of course it was quite fitting since Sebastian done both of those already. "You don't know how long I've waited to do that."

Elise laughed, "Ah, you mean since this morning, when you left."

"Every minute away from you feels like a lifetime," Sebastian winked.

"Now I know you both have been up to something. I only get a line like that, when you two have been up to something."

"Just visiting Mother. She sent some teacakes home with us," Gabriel answered, nodding at the basket he was carrying. "Sebastian was just going to help me get ready for my next trip."

"You're leaving again?" Elise asked. "It seems like you just got back."

"I heard about a village library that needs a statue." Gabriel replied.

"Well, you'll have hurry home with some more wonderful stories. How soon are you leaving?" she asked.

"Right away."

"No, Gabriel! You must at least stay for dinner. Leave first thing in the morning. I'm sure your journey can wait just a bit longer. I've made a lovely rabbit stew."

"I'd love to Elise, and I promise when I come back we'll have a celebration."

"I know it's pointless to argue with you, when you've found your inspiration, so go ahead and pack—and don't forget your fiddle this time—I know how you hate to be without it."

Gabriel followed Sebastian and Elise inside, the main door opened into quaint room with a stone fireplace, shelves full of copper pots and pans, and a large round table on which sat a clay pot full of flowers. Gabriel dropped the basket on the table and followed Elise into the two back rooms. "I washed your shirts. They should be sitting on your bed." Elise motioned toward the left door, which Gabriel supposed was his room.

"Gabriel, I need to speak with you before you leave," Sebastian said as he followed Elise into the other room.

"The whole world rearranges itself and yet he's still ordering me around," Gabriel muttered under his breath. Gabriel looked around the small room. It was warm and cozy with a narrow bed, a small dresser, an arched window that looked out into the garden, and a wooden trunk. Hanging on the wall was his fiddle. Gabriel opened the trunk and inside were all his tools. Grabbing his satchel, he began packing. Gabriel came upon the chisel--the one with ornate handle, the same one that had stabbed the Swamp Witch, carved the Ice

Maiden, and killed Sebastian. He looked at it closely and ran his fingers along it.

"Here, you never did any of those things. Here, everything is just the way it should be." Gabriel packed it in his satchel along with some clothing and his fiddle.

"There you are," said Elise. "I packed you some food for the road. Have a safe journey."

"Thank you." Gabriel responded, taking the basket from Elise and giving her a kiss on the cheek. "Don't let Sebastian order you around."

Elise let out a laugh. "I'm used to him, and he knows better than to tell me what to do. He saves that for you."

"I'll walk you out," Sebastian said dryly. Once they were out of the front door and beyond Elise's hearing, Sebastian continued. "You're going to see that Gypsy aren't you?"

"Yes, but I don't know if she'll remember me."

"Do you need me to go with you?" Sebastian asked.

"No, you belong here. You spent enough time miserable, now it's time for you to be happy. "

Sebastian shook his head. "Happy. Such an absurd concept for me. There's something I wanted to warn you about. My memories, they're already starting to change. I'm not sure how much we'll remember about our other past. You need to find her soon, before you forget you're looking for her."

"I don't think I can ever forget that I'm looking for her."

Sebastian smiled, "Ah dear brother, it sounds like you're in love."

"I'm afraid I am," Gabriel answered with a laugh.

"All right, so go find her, already." Sebastian gave him a hug. "And be safe."

"Be happy." Gabriel responded and walked toward the path away from town and into the country side.

"I knew it!" Johanna cried.

"You fixed it!" Casper called out.

"I didn't fix anything," Mrs. Kinder answered with indignance. "This is the way the story always goes."

"I've been waiting for this part for so long…when Gabriel meets the Gypsy again." Johanna answered.

"Well then my dear, I hope it's everything you wanted it to be," Mrs. Kinder answered.

Gabriel made the journey to the lemon village. His anxiousness made the trip seem longer, and as time passed, he understood more of what Sebastian had warned him about. His memories were starting to change, and the bad past, full of death and separation was becoming only a terrible dream that was slowly fading; even the Gypsy seemed more like a lovely dream than reality.

It was nighttime when he arrived at the familiar village and the sight of all the lemon trees in neat rows brought a smile to his face. He ran through the lemon village and straight to the inn. He walked through the door and into the adjoining pub. "She has to be here," he muttered to himself. Scanning the room, he didn't see a trace of her anywhere.

"What took you so long?" a familiar voice called out to him. A smile lit Gabriel's face and he turned to see the Gypsy standing there.

Gabriel walked up to her. "You remember?"

"I see you in all my dreams."

"Come with me," Gabriel said suddenly, grabbing her hand. He pulled her from the busy pub and out into the street.

"Where are we going," she asked breathlessly.

"The library."

"I don't think this is the time for books."

"Just trust me," Gabriel answered. He brought her to the library garden. The block of stone stood uncarved as though it were waiting for Gabriel. The Gypsy sat on the stone bench and Gabriel pulled his fiddle from his satchel. "My name is Gabriel and I'd like to play you a song." He lifted the fiddle and began to play. The song was full of love and yearning and the deepest hope, the same song he'd played for her that night they unveiled his statue. He finished the song and put down the fiddle.

"I know that song," she said. "I've heard it before."

Gabriel sat down beside her. "Yes."

"You said you'd come. In my dream, you promised you'd come back."

"Yes. And there's something important I've waited a long time to tell you. But there's one thing I need to know first… Your name?"

"My name? There's only one person who knows my name."

"Yes, your brother Brishen."

She looked startled. "Have you met him?" she asked. "If he told you, I'll kill him."

Gabriel laughed. "No, he didn't tell me. I wanted you to tell me."

"And I want you to know," she said. "My name is Faith."

"That's beautiful. My dearest Faith, you're going to think I'm mad. But I've learned that there is a world full of impossible things and this is the most impossible of all: with all my heart and soul, I love only you."

Faith reached over and took Gabriel's hand. "I've seen a lot of magic, but this is beyond what I'd ever thought to find, so as odd as it sounds Gabriel, I love you too."

Gabriel leaned over, took her in his arms, and kissed her in the way they write storybooks about.

EPILOGUE

"There are some things you wait so long for, that when you finally get them—they simply can't stand up to the amount of longing and want that's been poured into them. Gabriel had waited so long to kiss Faith, and when he kissed her—it was so much better than anything he'd imagined. And of course, my dears, they lived happily ever after."

"Mrs. Kinder, that was wonderful!" Johanna exclaimed.

"I guess the gross love stuff wasn't *too* bad," Casper admitted grudgingly.

Johanna gave him a look that said see-I-was-right-all-along.

"I'm sorry I said your story was horrible," he finished.

"That's quite all right Casper. Any storyteller worth their salt would be flattered someone cared so much about their tale." Mrs. Kinder answered.

At that moment, the doorbell rang.

"That must be your mother," said Mrs. Kinder, as she rose to answer the door with Johanna and Casper close behind her.

When Mrs. Kinder opened the door she was greeted by a smiling Emily Sullivan.

"Things went well?" Mrs. Kinder asked.

Emily stepped inside. "Yes." She turned to face the children "The surgery went well, and your Dad is recovering. It'll be a couple days before you can see him. I would have called but I wanted to tell you the good news in person."

"Yeah!" Casper yelled excitedly.

"When can Dad come home?" Johanna asked.

"They're not sure yet, but hopefully soon."

"That's wonderful news," said Mrs. Kinder.

"Did you guys have a good time today?" asked Emily.

"Yes! Mrs. Kinder has a cookie gun. A COOKIE gun!" said Casper. "Those are like my two favorite words put together."

Emily laughed. "How about you Johanna?"

"Yes. Mrs. Kinder finished her story and it was wonderful. Plus, she knew great-grandmother Liesel."

"Really?" Emily answered and turned to face Mrs. Kinder.

"She was my sitter for one afternoon, long ago— although some days it seems just like yesterday." Mrs. Kinder pulled off her glasses and rubbed them on her apron, then placed them back on her nose. "You get old and long ago and just yesterday turn into the same thing. I recommend staying young as long as possible."

"I just wanted to thank you again for watching the children these last couple days."

"Just returning a favor," Mrs. Kinder answered, her eyes twinkling.

"Still it was really kind of you, and it helped our family so much. Once Henry is feeling better, I'd love to have you over for dinner."

"That would be lovely dear."

"Are you guys ready to go home?" asked Emily.

"Yes!" said Casper eagerly as he gathered up his things.

"I guess," Johanna answered.

"Would it be all right if Johanna stayed a little longer?" Mrs. Kinder asked. "There's something I'd like to show her. It'll only be a few minutes or so, and I'll watch to make sure she gets home safe."

"Fine with me. How about you Johanna?" Emily asked.

"Sure," Johanna answered.

"Okay honey, I'll see you in a little while. Goodnight Mrs. Kinder, and thanks again."

"Don't mention it."

Casper turned to look at Johanna and whisper, "I think you're stupid, very stupid—but if you turn into a frog, I'll make sure you have a really nice aquarium." And with that, Casper joined Emily and they left Mrs. Kinder's house.

Mrs. Kinder shut the door and it closed with a click that seemed unusually loud to Johanna.

"Wha—What did you want to show me?" Johanna asked, annoyed with the momentary twinge of fear that pulsed through her.

"Follow me."

Johanna pushed aside that bit of apprehension still left. Mrs. Kinder had only ever been kind to her and she was determined to show the same kindness in return. She had decided, that sometimes being brave just meant deciding to see the best in people.

Mrs. Kinder let her back to the sitting room, to where she'd left the golden book. She opened the pages and pulled something out and handed it to Johanna.

Johanna took it in her hand and realized it was a photograph of two girls, about Johanna's age. They looked exactly the same.

"That's a photograph of your great grandmother Liesel and your great aunt Johanna."

"Really?" Johanna said in wonder, her eyes growing wider. "How did you get this?"

"Your great grandmother sent it to me."

"Because you reminded her of her sister?" asked Johanna.

"Yes and I think because my name is also Johanna."

Johanna Sullivan let out a surprised gasp while Johanna Kinder laughed.

"She told me that Johannas should always stick together and she sent me one other thing. This." Mrs. Kinder turned to pick up the golden book. "And I'd like to give it to you."

Johanna's hand shook a bit as she opened it, and once she did, she felt a surge of disappointment. "It's blank!" she exclaimed. "There's nothing on any of the pages!"

"Turn to the last one," Mrs. Kinder answered.

Johanna Sullivan did just that, and when she reached the very back of the book there was a note written in black ink, in lovely curled script.

Write your own story

and make it the most wonderful adventure you

can imagine.

And love – make sure it always ends with love,

the best stories always do.

- Liesel

Johanna ran her fingers over the letters.

"I think she gave me this book and this photograph, so one day I'd give it to you."

"How would she know that?" Johanna Sullivan asked.

"There's all kinds of magic in the world—all kinds. Not knowing *how* something happens doesn't make it any less true."

"The story you told Casper and me—was that your story or her story?"

Mrs. Kinder smiled, "Does it really matter?" She placed her hand on Johanna's shoulder. "After awhile, all our stories they run into each other—we all become a part of each other. How much of your great grandmother Liesel's story was her sister Johanna's? And how much of your story will be a part of mine? Or your parents? Or Casper's?"

Johanna paused to consider this and nodded at Mrs. Kinder. "You're really giving this to me?"

"Of course, it's your turn. Besides, we Johannas need to stick together, remember?"

"Thank you." Johanna continued, a note of hesitance in her voice, "Would it be okay if I gave you a hug goodbye?"

"I'd like that very much," Mrs. Kinder said. Johanna reached over and hugged Mrs. Kinder, and noticed she smelled a bit like oranges and flowers.

"Thank you," Johanna whispered.

Johanna Kinder walked Johanna Sullivan to the front door and let the girl onto the front porch.

"Would it be okay if I came some other afternoon and we could tell some more stories?" Johanna asked.

"As you wish," Mrs. Kinder responded with a nod.

Johanna smiled and brightly said, "Goodnight" and ran across the street to her home.

Mrs. Kinder watched her carefully and when Johanna Sullivan reached her front door, she gave a wave. Mrs. Kinder smiled and waved back. Then, she shut the door behind her, humming a familiar melody.

~ The End ~

ACKNOWLEDGEMENTS

Every story has another story behind it. "The Ice Maiden's Tale" started a very long time ago, in a cold and frozen kingdom. I was a freshman at Syracuse University and found my way into George Saunders' sophomore Fiction Writing Workshop. As is the way with college level writing courses, most students were trying to create the most shocking or experimental prose they could. I found myself the night before I needed to submit my writing for class critique, with absolutely nothing ready. I kept a file of famous quotations for inspiration and decided to flip through it. I came across a quote by Michelangelo, "I saw an angel in the marble, and I carved until I set him free."   In a flash, there was a story. I stayed up most of the night and when I stopped typing there was a fairy tale.

I prepared myself for a torturous critique, imagining how my edgy classmates and brilliant professor would react to a children's story. Surprisingly, nearly everyone liked it. It was a short story then, just a few pages, but I used it to get into the Senior Fiction Writing workshop with Robert O'Connor--the class helped me fulfil my final requirement for a Creative Writing minor.

I graduated, years past, and life went on. Then, I decided to pursue an MFA in Creative Writing. I applied to the New School, which happened to have a "Writing for Children" concentration in their Fiction program. I had written a children's story, so I figured, why not submit it? And that same story, earned me a place at the New School and in one of the best Creative Writing programs in the country.

While at The New School, I studied with some incredible professors including Tor Seidler, Sarah Weeks and David Levithan. It was in David Levithan's literature class about dark and light in children's books, that it clicked on how to turn my tiny fairy tale into something bigger. That short story turned into a novel that turned into my graduate creative thesis for which my advisor, Susan Van Metre, gave her fabulous expertise to help shape. Along the way I was privileged enough to be a part of the most amazing writer's group in the history of ever: Maude Bonde, Amalia Ellison, Lucas Klauss, Morgan Matson, and Zach Miller. They, along with my classmate Camilia Phillips, are all phenomenally talented and left their mark on this story.

After graduation, I tried to get this book published, but despite lots of positive feedback from agents, it was just a little too different, a little too old fashioned—a little too hard to sell, so I put it aside and tried to work on other things. More years passed, and then one day, I saw a posting by Michael Dobbs looking for middle-grade submissions for Xist Publishing. I figured I had a finished novel, why not take a chance? She and Calee Lee, offered me the opportunity to finally let this story do was it always meant to – be read by children. Michael Dobbs edits helped make this story shine and Calee's determination helped it find an audience. My deepest thanks to Calee for helping me realize my dream of publication and to her daughter, Audrey, the first child to read this book, for her thoughtful advice and encouragement.

As you can imagine a story that took 19 years to find its way into the world, requires a great deal more gratitude. So here I go:

.

To Sabrina Marchal, who believed in me (and this story) when I had long since given up. I'm not sure it would have made it this far without her.

To my Mom, Clementina Preziosi, without whose help I would never have been able to study creative writing and get my degrees. Without her, my stories would have stopped before they started.

To my Nonna in Italy, Pasqualina Preziosi, who has never once failed to send me a card for my birthday. Your thoughtfulness circumvents any distance.

To my big sister Maria Preziosi Pope, my Aunt Terry Preziosi and all my cousins and relatives close and far – Thank you for your support and inspiration.

To my best friend, Preethi Nair– I could have spent my life trying to write the perfect best friend to have adventures (and misadventures) with and never come close. Thanks for always saying "yes" to my crazy suggestions. It made my life and my stories so much better.

To all my close friends, in real life and online, for their laughs and support and endless patience. There is no way I could possibly thank everyone who touched this story (or my heart) over the years. Some of you I speak to daily and others I've lost touch, but you've left a mark on me and this book and I'd be remiss if I didn't mention you: Cecilia Eng, Rosanna Camporeale,

Jose Martinez, BBR, Mike Errickson, Stacey Ohl, Michael Chiong, Noelia Nagode, Carolina Parker and Vittoria Caputi – Thank you.

To all the wonderful children in my life that I've watched grow up, including: Jack and Abigail Pope, Naveen and Naina Martinez, Kingston Eng, Alyssa and AJ D'Angelo, Liam and Logan Gohde, Madeline Gomez, Azariah, Emma and Toni Preziosi, Emilia and Elise Sonneman – you remind me why children are the absolute best people to write for.

And of course, to my partner in crime and life, David Austin, for supporting me through the rejection, the work, the hours behind a closed door and all the crazy business that comes with being a writer.

I love all of you. You are the soul inside my stories.

Thank you.

CPSIA information can be obtained
at www.ICGtesting.com
Printed in the USA
FSOW01n0502281017
40296FS